New Fiction

Let The Tale Begin . . . A Collection Of Short Stories For Children

Edited by

Steve Twelvetree

First published in Great Britain in 2004 by
NEW FICTION
Remus House,
Coltsfoot Drive,
Peterborough, PE2 9JX
Telephone (01733) 898101
Fax (01733) 313524

SB ISBN 1 85929 105 8

FOREWORD

When 'New Fiction' ceased publishing there was much wailing and gnashing of teeth, the showcase for the short story had offered an opportunity for practitioners of the craft to demonstrate their talent.

Phoenix-like from the ashes, 'New Fiction' has risen with the sole purpose of bringing forth new and exciting short stories from new and exciting writers.

The art of the short story writer has been practised from ancient days, with many gifted writers producing small, but hauntingly memorable stories that linger in the imagination.

I believe this selection of stories will leave echoes in your mind for many days. Read on and enjoy the pleasure of that most perfect form of literature, the short story.

Parvus Est Bellus.

Contents

The Onion, The Cauliflower And The Bee

Del Isaacs

Once upon a time there was a sweet little onion growing in a man's garden. Although the onion was quite happy, he would have liked to be a bit larger so that the children in the garden could see him better and would not tread on him.

There was also a cauliflower in the man's garden. She was much bigger than the little onion and in fact, it was because of her that the onion was so small. You see, because the cauliflower was so big, she cast a shadow over the poor onion so that the onion never saw the sunshine.

The little onion and the cauliflower didn't know that the sun makes you grow.

One day a busy bee came buzzing by and sat for a rest on the little onion.

'Please don't sit on me,' cried the little onion, 'you're so heavy and I'm so small.'

'I am sorry,' said the bee, 'you are very small. Would you like me to help you to grow?'

'Ooh, that would be very nice, but how could you help me to grow?'

'Well you see,' said the bee, 'the reason you don't grow is that you don't have enough sunshine. If I can bring you some sunshine and sprinkle it over you, you will soon start to grow.'

'But how will you collect sunshine?' said the little onion. 'You can't catch it and put it in a box.'

'Leave that to me,' said the bee. 'Now I must get busy, byeee, zzz.'

Off went the bee, flying this way and that and zigzagging over all the gardens till he came to his secret place. At his secret place was a tall sunflower.

She swayed to and fro and waved hello to the busy bee. 'Have you come for some of my sunshine to make some honey?'

'I've come for some of your sunshine, but not to make honey,' he buzzed, and he told the story of the little onion.

After the story was told, the sunflower smiled and said, 'I'll be happy to help the little onion.'

So the bee took some sunshine from the sunflower and flew off back to the man's garden where the little onion and the big cauliflower lived.

'Hello little onion,' cried the bee, 'and hello big cauliflower.'

'Hello Mr Bee,' said the little onion, 'have you managed to bring me some sunshine?'

'I certainly have,' said the bee, and he started to sprinkle the golden yellow dust all over the little onion.

'Mind you don't blow some on me!' said the big cauliflower. 'It wouldn't do for me to get any bigger.'

'Ha, ha, ha!' they all laughed.

The busy bee brought sunshine to the little onion for seven days. By which time, the little onion had grown so much that he could see the sunshine over the cauliflower so did not need the bee's services any longer.

Two weeks went by and the bee came back to see the little onion, who by now was very much larger, and much prettier.

'My, you have changed,' said the bee.

'Yes, and it's all thanks to you and your sunshine,' said the little onion. 'But what can I do for you in return?'

'You don't know it but you have done something for me. Look at yourself, you're a lovely tulip, you weren't an onion at all, but a tulip bulb. Now I can come to see you for sunshine powder and give Ms Sunflower a rest.'

'Yes, and I have something better to look at than an onion,' said the big cauliflower.

So they all lived happily in the man's garden ever after.

GARY'S LAW

Liz DiMarcello

Rosie and Odie whispered to each other quietly. They had to talk like this, otherwise the 'people' would hear them. The two girls didn't want the 'people' to listen to what they were planning.

It didn't really matter though, because Rosie and Odie were gerbils. The 'people' can't understand the gerbil secret language, which is just as well. You see, these two gerbil girls were up to no good. They were planning an escape. The one thing that stood in their way was big, black and furry. Gary the cat.

Gary is a legend in all of gerbil history. Stories of his terrible claws, and the speed he could run at, followed every gerbil through its life. The girls had to be very careful to pack their little cases quietly. Rosie shut the lid on her case, and zipped it up slowly. She let out a breath of relief that she'd made no noise. When Odie tried to zip her case up it caught the end of her tail in the bag. She tried hard not to cry. Gary was lying close by, fast asleep. The last thing they wanted to do was wake him up!

The gerbils' cases were small enough for them to carry the handles in their mouths. They wrote their names on the little labels in the cases. Well, they didn't want to lose all their cotton socks, did they?

Odie got the door of their cage undone by pulling at the catch with her tail. She was the smart one of the pair. Rosie was a lot better at doing things more than thinking about things. Rosie said to Odie, 'Uh, do you think we'll get past Gary?'

Odie answered, 'Of course we shall dear, do have faith in me a little!'

Rosie was still worried. 'What about the people?'

'They're watching television, they'll never see us,' Odie said.

'They never see us anyway.' Rosie was upset as she was reminded of the reason for leaving the cage. 'They don't play with us anymore, I don't think they like us now.'

Odie tried to make her sister feel better. 'I know Rosie, they did like us once though. Do you remember all those times they played with us when we were young?'

'Yes, I remember,' said Rosie, 'I can't see why they like that computer games thing better than us, can you?'

Odie couldn't either. 'I don't understand it,' she said.

It was true, since the 'people' had got the computer thing they hadn't played with the girls anymore.

Feeling sad and hurt the girls jumped down from the table top onto the floor. Then, all of a sudden they heard a nasty hissing sound behind them! It was Gary! He'd been listening to everything they had said. He was just as scary as the girls had heard he was. They squeaked in fright and ran under a shoe.

Gary tapped at the shoe, trying to knock it over. Rosie cried out, 'Please don't hurt us Mr Pussycat Gary Sir!'

Odie shouted, 'We're only going to find a better home, please let us go!'

Gary, being a cat, was smart enough to understand what they were saying. As you know, cats are smarter than 'people'.

Gary spoke slowly, so the girls could hear him properly. 'Let me tell you something about the 'people'. I rule the house, not them. Oh they may think they know what's going on in here, but I'm the only one with power enough to do something. You could say that I am the 'law'. I'll deal with your problem.' He smiled widely, showing his sharp white teeth. 'Now,' Gary purred, 'tell me all about it.'

So Rosie and Odie told Gary how they felt and he listened carefully to it all. When they stopped, Rosie said, 'Perhaps you could make them like us again?'

Gary twitched his whiskers for a while. Then he said, 'Yes, I think I have an idea. Stay here and whatever you do, don't move!'

The girls were too scared to do anything. They crept back under the shoe.

Gary walked into the 'people's' room. He held his head high and moved round behind the chairs. Once he was ready, he crouched down and got ready to jump.

There was some food and a glass of drink on top of the television. Perfect for Gary's plan. With one single leap, the cat jumped straight onto the plate of food, knocking everything flying.

The 'people' were so shocked that they ran out of the room screaming in fright! The youngest of them, a little boy, kicked over the gerbils' shoe.

'Mummy, Mummy,' yelled the little boy, 'look what I've found!'

The woman bent down to pick up the gerbils. She picked up Rosie and handed her to the boy. 'Now you be careful with her Tommy, she's only little.'

Tommy looked happily at Rosie. He said to his mum, 'Rosie's lovely Mummy, can I play with her a while?'

'Of course you can,' said his mum. 'I'll play with Odie.'

Odie smiled up at Tommy's mum.

'Perhaps they've been lonely,' the woman said.

Gary looked out of the window. All was right with the world again.

Tartan Scarves

F D Gunn

Grrrrrr, was that her alarm clock already? Beth had been out partying all night and still felt drunk when the DJ on her bedside radio alarm clock announced cheerily and a bit too loudly that it was 6.30am. Beth groaned, pulled the duvet over her head, turned over and tried to forget that another long, boring shift in the factory was her exciting fate for today.

This was the life of a student on her summer holidays. Slowly pulling herself to a sitting position Beth considered getting up, then deciding she deserved five minutes more, she flopped back on her pillow. Over half an hour later she reluctantly dragged herself out of bed. Accepting that another 'Groundhog Day' had begun.

No time to shower, she sniffed her armpits and rolled on some extra-strength deodorant.

'Happy talk, keep talkin', happy talkin' . . .' she sang as she made the short trip to MacLinsay's mill that made tartan for distribution worldwide. She could hear the sound of the looms at work as she turned into Melrose Terrace.

There were a few girls in overalls outside the gates. These were the full time workers who in general worked very hard and had become skilled at their mind-numbingly boring jobs.

'Good morning Bethhh,' wheezed Ethel, the oldest of the bunch.

'Hi ladies, nice morning. Anyone know the time? I forgot my watch.' Beth gushed.

With a few minutes to spare she chatted to Mrs Liddell, one of the office staff. Mrs Liddell was very regal in demeanour and could often be seen wearing fancy hats in the supermarket.

Beth heard the chatter of girls arriving to start the day and knew it was time to clock in.

She then stood at her position around the makeshift table along with her workmates, poised to begin the exciting task of folding and bagging scarves of varying colours.

There were several big decisions to make, she could either fold the fabric neatly around the cardboard, use the metal chute to help bag them at speed, move at speed to box them. Quickly she stood, Afro-comb in hand, ready to fold the first batch of the day.

The boys from the storeroom and the factory manager, Victor, dumped them on the table.

'Yippee, Black Watch Tartan, my favourite,' she groaned at no one in particular.

One of Beth's closest friends and fellow science student walked in.

'Morning Judith, have you sobered up yet?'

'Almost, put the radio on hon, will you?'

It was right on the tip of Beth's tongue to ask her what her last slave died of, but realised Judith was suffering the effects of one too many vodkas.

In stumbled Sharon. What a sight! Beth smiled. Sharon was a permanent fixture in the factory. She was a fashion victim, always caked in orange fake tan and usually singing, 'Ebenezer's good'.

'Someone turn that s**t off, my heid's bumping,' she said.

They all looked at Judith, knowing she would speak up.

'Several of us have headaches Sharon, but we still want the radio on,' Jude replied.

The room fell silent, was there going to be a fight? Sensing trouble Nicola, a small Chinese girl, began to clatter about loudly, cleverly causing much distraction. And so the morning started.

Shortly after, Victor, the factory manager, introduced a new girl to swell the ranks. Anne was a physiotherapy student. She was extremely bubbly and sadly excited about her new job.

Beth still a bit weary thought, *If I hear that stupid laugh once more, she is going home with her teeth in her pocket.*

'Here Anne, stand here and I'll show you what to do.'

The girls chattered away all morning and quickly became friends.

It was soon lunchtime, there were no official breaks, although there were several unofficial toilet and fag breaks.

Judith, Beth and their new pal Anne popped into the staff canteen to buy diet Cokes. Nelly, a pretty stout girl, was there with her diet milkshake. Poor, poor Nelly was often seen gorging on chip shop chips.

Leaving the hot, dusty environment the three girls left to sit on the wall outside the factory gates and eat their packed lunches.

'Phew, that's another few orders done. I hope Victor is satisfied,' said Beth.

'How many do we need to do?'

'I couldn't say for sure Anne pal, Victor is happy and that's the main thing. We do what we're told, follow ridiculous rules and get on with things,' Beth answered.

'Yeah, the high point of the day is getting a different tartan to fold,' adds Jude.

The girls laughed.

'So what are you doing tonight Beth?' asked Anne.

'Well, Jude and I were out on the Ramadan last night until the early hours, so I think it's a long bath and an early night for me.'

Judith, who had recently got her nose pierced, complained about the nuisance it caused when she wanted to blow her nose.

'Remove it, or quit moaning,' said Beth.

'Who made you boss all of a sudden?' retorted Judith.

Refusing to be defeated, she stuck her tongue out. 'Time to go girls,' she said.

'Already?' moaned Anne.

'Yeah, only half an hour, factory hours,' said Jude getting up.

Wearily the three young girls trailed back up the staircase to return to their table.

'I am so tired, think anyone would notice if I had a snooze under the table?' asked Beth.

Judith laughed at her funny friend.

Their fellow worker, Caroline, joined them. Equally funny and determined to lift the girls' spirits, she had pulled up the hood of her grey top and made a cardboard sign saying, 'Help the homeless, please give generously.' She sat cross-legged next to a packing box. Students and workers alike howled with laughter at her antics.

'Get up, you nutcase.' Beth pulled her friend to her feet.

The girls continued with their monotonous work, alternating between playing word games, having dancing competitions (which Sharon always wanted to win).

'Right girls, let's play guess who I am,' said Beth.

'Yes,' agreed Judith.

'Not again,' said Caroline.

'I'm not playin',' said Sharon moodily.

'Moody cow!'

'OK, let's go!' Anne responded emphatically.

This was how the girls passed the boring days. They created a party atmosphere in their otherwise drab surroundings. The students were perhaps the most overdramatic, but there were several characters among them, especially the older of crowd. There was Olive Oil and her younger sister Bridget, whose previous day's knickers had just fallen out the leg of her jeans. How embarrassing! What a laugh!

'Shhh,' said Beth, seeing Victor approaching them.

Victor seemed quite intimidated by the chattering girls. However, he always said his piece, usually inserting several swear words.

He crept up. 'Do you girls realise that we have 16 new orders to do by Friday?'

'What's that Victor?' Sharon grinned cheekily.

'You heard me Sharon, stop the chatting and get on with the work.'

'Sure thing Victor,' said Jude, grabbing her next scarf for folding.

Victor left.

'Moaning bastard,' said Sharon.

'Phew, that was close,' said Beth.

The girls industriously continued their work.

'I'm tired,' Anne stopped.

'Can't we sit down to work?' she asked.

''Fraid not, to be honest, it's easier to work standing up,' said Beth.

'But those girls have stools,' she nodded in the direction of the next room.

'They're the pickers,' said Caroline.

'What do they do?'

'Not much,' Sharon said.

Beth smiled and answers, 'They pick any flaws out in the fabric.'

'Must be hard on the eyes,' Anne commented.

'Mmm, boring too,' commented Beth, continuing to comb the tassels on the scarves.

The afternoon continued without much event. There were times of silence, times of much noise and laugher interrupted by visits by management asking them to keep the noise down and turn the volume of the radio down.

Beth was looking around the room, wondering why only girls were employed here and boys in the storeroom. Why were all the cleaners women? And you seldom saw a man with a duster in his hand. Sighing and deciding that was just life, she got on with things.

The siren marked the end of the day and the girls wearily trudged to the clocking machine.

'So, will we see you tomorrow Anne?' asked Jude.

'Of course,' she replied with enthusiasm.

The working day over, Beth trudged the short distance home. 'Home, home, home, is where the heart beats,' she hummed.

'Hi Mum,' she yelled as she passed through the steamy kitchen. 'What's for dinner?'

Her mum looked very flushed from the heat. 'Hi darling, it's fish tonight. Do you want some?'

'Just a small bit, please. Are the boys in?'

Beth had two younger brothers, Iain and Fraser.

'Fraser's in, Iain's not.'

She raced upstairs to her room. *I'm so tired,* she thought as she swiped all the clutter off her bed so she could play dead for 4.4667 seconds.

Time up, she headed back downstairs carrying an assortment of used plates and nearly new clothes, to bask in the aroma of freshly-cooked mayonnaise. Oh, and the cod fish dish. Luverlie!

The Little Dime

(For my great nephews Micheal and David Rennie)
Gerard Allardyce

The summer lingered that year in 1901. The sun shone strong and beautiful over Lake Champlain where Chris, twelve, and his little companion Jennifer, eleven, were boating and fishing. It was perhaps fortunate that the bubbly Vice-President of the United States decided that he would like to take a boat out from the Isle La Motte. Perhaps he too would enjoy a bit of fishing.

'I'm goddamn sure that the President won't die from the hands of that assassin . . . I'm quite sure about that, but I will go to Buffalo when I think the occasion demands.'

Chris was rowing the old boat meanwhile, unaware it was leaking water slowly beneath him and little Jennifer. For every trout they caught at this, the Vermont Fish and Game League, the boat lay heavier in the water.

She cried out as the calm lake suddenly looked dangerous. 'Oh Chris . . . the boat!'

'Must get something out of all this,' Chris said, stuffing a trout in his shirt as a wave sunk the old rowing boat.

'Oh Chris, I'm frightened.'

'We'll be alright Jennifer.' But Chris knew that the currents of Lake Champlain were dangerous and the water cold. Jennifer was a poor swimmer and of course, he supported her as only he knew how and dreaded the current that could sweep them under.

Teddy's little cruiser had just left the island and Teddy was in no mood to suffer advice meekly.

'I tell you, the President will live, so don't let's worry about it.' Then, 'Hey Jake, don't you think we should turn back to the island? Hey look there, two kiddies in the water . . . let's get them aboard . . . then I could do with a brandy, but those kiddies there . . . well come on Jake, let's go, go, go.'

There were strong sailors on the little vessel and they helped with nets to bring Chris and Jennifer to safety.

'Mr Vice-President Sir, the name's Chris, and the girl Jennifer . . . we're mighty pleased to see you and your boat.'

‘Well Chris, I’m a big boy . . . a rough rider . . . you saved that little girl’s life.’

‘We were fishing when our boat sank Sir, but here’s a fish we caught . . . a lovely rainbow trout for you and your family.’

‘Well, that is goddamn nice of you son, and in return, I’ll give you this silver dime for old time’s sake. Remember son, that fools and their money are always parted. Now when you get ashore, go back to your family and remember your dear old Vice-president, whom a moment ago became President of the United States of America upon the tragic death of Mr McKinley.’

Jennifer and Chris grew up to love this man second only to their own families. Teddy, as President and Elder Statesman, held their affections. Jennifer, remembering the steamboat in Lake Champlain, had two Teddies. One named Chris, the boy she loved and was to marry and of course, Teddy, the Teddy of all American armchair fame.

As for Chris, he kept the little silver dime for luck in his pocket watch cover.

This was to be the next meeting. It was 1912 and Teddy was addressing an election rally for his bid once again to ascend the Presidency. Chris and Jennifer were right there to see the great man himself run for President. They were outside the Hotel Gilpatrick in Milwaukee. They saw him speak, then sway and speak again with difficulty. Nothing it seemed could stop Teddy in full flow, but Chris and Jennifer slipped away to the store. They bought a bottle of brandy for the great man, spending the silver dime in the process.

‘I don’t think Teddy has been badly hurt, but we must get ready to see him in hospital . . . he’s been shot . . . Jennifer . . . he’s speaking . . . he’s speaking.’

‘I will make this speech or die. It is one thing or the other . . .’

Then, of course, Chris’ dad had been a Senator and that with a pass and bottle, both Chris and Jennifer found Teddy in hospital.

'The kids in the water, Lake Champlain 1901 . . . little silver dime, lovely rainbow trout for me and my wife Edith . . . but you spent the little silver dime . . . the brandy . . . ah well, let's celebrate and enjoy at my home with all our families a hundred-dollar meal . . . delighted, charmed, but you know something? It was the little dime that brought us together and so remember, 'one good turn deserves another,' and Teddy sat up jubilant in his bed.

PIGS MIGHT FLY

Doreen Roberts

Storm clouds were gathering when they left Aunt Dottie's house to take her darling pet for his walkies. There were few people about in such weather. Ben and his cousin Lucy seemed to be in the wrong place at the wrong time. They were staying with their aunt for the weekend, whilst both sets of parents were away on business. The two children were stopped in their tracks by a flash of lightning, followed by a clap of thunder and heavy rain. They were too late. 'He' had discovered the forbidden tree and was sniffing and snuffling in its roots. Porodos had escaped by pulling his head from the dog collar, running off, leaving Ben trailing an empty lead.

'We've got to catch him, hurry, we must get him or we're in for it,' shouted Ben breathlessly.

'I can't run much faster,' gasped Lucy. 'The rain is stinging my face.'

Aunt Dottie would be cross; she had given them strict orders to keep away from the large mulberry tree. Porodos seemed to like it. Whilst he was rummaging in the roots, Ben managed to fasten the dog collar around his neck. Another brilliant flash, with an awesome crack of thunder, hit the tree, leaving a cleft in its trunk.

Porodos was inside the inviting hole before one could say, 'Porodos is a pig,' which he was. A black, pot-bellied pig that Aunt Dottie adored and fussed over like a spoilt child. She assured everyone that he was well house-trained; even so, people stayed away, which pleased Aunt Dottie. She was Dottie by name and dotty by nature. Ben struggled to pull Porodos out of the split tree. Lucy held onto Ben by his sweater.

'Oh don't, don't Lucy, you are strangling me, let go,' he gurgled.

As Lucy released the sweater, Porodos gave a strong tug on the lead, dragging Ben into the hollow. They rolled over and down a grassy slope bathed in brilliant warm sunshine. Lucy stood alone amongst the tree roots for a moment, staring into the opening until her inquisitive nature got the better of her. With trepidation she stooped to investigate the dark place, carefully she stepped inside. At her third step she slipped, to tumble downwards ending her strange journey beside Ben and Porodos on the warm grass.

'Wow,' said Ben, 'this is cool, what do you think Lucy?'

‘I’ll tell you when my head stops spinning. It’s amazing, where are we?’

‘Dunno,’ replied Ben. ‘We can ask Aunt Dottie when we get home. She must know about this place, that’s why she ordered us to keep away from the mulberry tree.’

‘You said when we get home Ben, but how do we get home?’

Both children, with Porodos snoring loudly, sat to review the incredible situation they had landed in.

‘We are surrounded by a circle of some sort, look at the strange earth mound round us,’ said Lucy.

‘Wicked,’ said Ben. ‘Now look at those weird creatures staring at us. What are they?’

‘Fantastic,’ squealed Lucy. ‘They look like aliens from space with pig snouts. I love the silver capes on their shoulders.’

‘Keep still and quiet,’ ordered Ben in a half-whisper. ‘Let them make the first move.’

Porodos stopped snoring. As they watched in fascination, he writhed and twisted, his body taking on almost human form. His black pig face remained. He raised his hands to his neck to remove the lead Ben was holding. Now dressed in a large black cape, with a cardboard crown on his head, he smiled to show two sabre teeth curling from his bottom jaw up and over his top piggy lip.

He spoke, ‘I am Porodoth, the thupreme thovereign of Mulberry Land. Welcome to you. My army of pigth that thurround you will therve you well. You may wander at will, accompanied at all timeth by a pig. Your needth will be thatithfied. There ith one thing you thoud know from the thtart. You can never leave thith plathe unleth you can tell uth how pigth might fly.’

Ben and Lucy sat staring in disbelief. Had they wandered into some sort of weird dream? They were surrounded by pig-faced guards watching their every move; with a large pot-bellied pig giving his orders with a lisp, spitting showers of piggy dribble over everything in range. The children sniggered at what they saw.

‘Have you gone bananas Porodos?’ shouted Ben, feeling slightly bemused.

A shushing noise came from Lucy. ‘Keep quiet Ben. Look over there, who’s that wafting this way?’

Both children stared open mouthed; it was Aunt Dottie in a black cape identical to the one Porodos wore.

'I see you could not carry out my orders,' she thundered. 'Now you must pay for your stupidity.'

Aunt Dottie sounded quite mean. The pale brown, jelly-like mole on the side of her chin, from which sprouted three long ginger hairs, wobbled up and down as she spoke.

'Is this some stupid joke, Auntie?' giggled Lucy as she observed with fascination the three long ginger hairs twitching in the breeze.

'Certainly not. I am mistress of Mulberry Land; I answer to my Lord Porodos. If you cannot tell us how pigs might fly, then you stay here forever.'

Ben laughed loudly. 'Is this some sort of amateur dramatics you are doing, Auntie?' he asked, suppressing another giggle.

'No, you horrid noisy children, this is no joking matter. Mulberry Land is here to save all pigs. We must know how to make them fly, so those held captive can be given the secret to help them escape from the hundreds of awful pig huts spread around the countryside, where they are fattened to face certain death to satisfy the human desire for their flesh.'

With a swirl of cloaks, Porodos, the lisping supreme sovereign, and his mistress Aunt Dottie marched away.

She turned to shout, 'Find a solution or stay where you are.'

The two children stared around helplessly, should they laugh or cry? Ben stood hoping to see more of Mulberry Land, as he did the army of pigs stood; when he sat down they followed his lead hiding behind the circle of earth.

'This is ridiculous and stupid,' said Lucy. 'What can we do Ben?'

'Sit here and think I suppose, I knew we would be in for it when Porodos ran off. What is our dotty auntie up to? This is like cartoon land.'

'Think Ben, how could we make a pig fly?'

'Kick him hard up his behind, I suppose, or hang him from a helicopter.'

'How would a pig find a helicopter?' asked Lucy.

Both children stood, the pig guards stood; Ben and Lucy walked close together around the inside of the earth mound. An army of piggy eyes followed them. The children were silent, then Ben said a wrong word. 'I'm starving; I could kill for a bacon sarnie!'

The pigs immediately picked up purple plastic guns, each fired a volley of juicy red mulberries at the astonished children.

'Stop it you rotten pigs,' shouted Ben. The pig army ducked behind their earth barrier.

'Ugh, what a stinking mess we are in, look at your red juicy hair Ben.'

Ben yelled back, 'Look at your own; it's Aunt Dottie's fault, the stupid old bag. I can't believe my mother is her sister.'

'Mine too, little wonder they seldom visit the batty old thing.'

'This place is not as funny as I first thought,' said Ben. He wiped the juice from his face with the back of his hands. They found a clean area of grass to sit and put on their thinking caps.

'I suppose we could tape wings to a pig's back, or wind up its stupid little tail and let go,' said Lucy.

'I thought of pogo sticks, but pigs could not hold them with their little trotters. Perhaps a giant catapult would do it. Come on Lucy, we are going to see Aunt Dottie and Porodos now, to demand they let us out of this freaky place.'

The two children left the circle accompanied by a pig guard. Amongst some trees they discovered a large pig sty, inside Aunt Dottie and her pet pig were relaxing. They sat in high-back cane chairs; she was feeding the dribbling Porodos chocolate buttons and jelly babies.

'We have come to ask your permission to leave this place Aunt Dottie; it's illegal to hold children against their will, so you had better say yes.'

'Shut up you grubby children, speak only if you have found an answer.'

'We have a few ideas,' as she spoke, Lucy hid behind Ben.

'Thpeak up, thay what you have to thay, then thut up. I exthpect it'th thomething thtupid,' lisped the black pig.

As Aunt Dottie laughed, the agitated mole moved up and down whipping its ginger hairs to and fro.

Ben spoke. 'Perhaps glue on some wings; or wind up the curly tail tight like a spring, maybe do both together.'

'Absurd! The tail is too small and glued-on wings would come adrift in the rain. Try again you stupid oafs, your mothers think you are so wonderful and would not expect you to be outwitted by pigs,' Aunt Dottie laughed mockingly.

'Perhaps pogo sticks might help?' said Lucy, cowering behind Ben.

'Utter nonsense,' bawled Auntie.

'You could try large catapults,' said Ben nervously.

'Prepothterouth, they would thuffer theriouth conthequentheth if they hit a hard thurfathe,' replied the pig. As he lisped, chocolate-coloured spit showered over the children.

'You're a disgusting pig!' screamed Lucy. Ben pulled his cousin away before Aunt Dottie or Porodos could retaliate. They hurried back to the circle.

'Listen Lucy, I have an idea, it suddenly came to me, but I wish I wasn't so hungry: I could murder a pork pie.'

Ben had done it again. A double volley of juicy mulberries splattered around them; in exasperation Lucy screamed more pig insults.

'Pork sausages, pork scratchings!' Ben joined her.

'Bacon flavoured crisps, ham and roast pork with crackling!'

The mulberries rained down upon them, so much had been fired the fruity ammunition was soon gone.

'What's this wonderful idea?' asked Lucy as she pushed red-stained hair from her face.

'Think, what flies without an engine and what makes it fly?'

Lucy thought. 'A balloon that uses gas! How can we fill a pig with gas? We would have to stick a tube up its . . .'

'No don't say it Lucy! The pigs must be fed a mixture of baked beans, Brussel sprouts and cabbage!' said Ben excitedly.

'With strong curry,' suggested Lucy. 'In fact, anything that will fill a pig full of wind. That sounds good Ben. I'd hate to be behind them when they backfire; ugh!'

'Cool,' said Ben. 'Stir in lager to make a pong-filled explosive mixture. Let's go back to the dotty aunt and Porodos.'

Auntie Dottie accepted the idea with interest. 'That's the best suggestion yet. If it does not work, then you will find yourselves prisoners in Mulberry Land once again.'

'How do we get back?' asked Ben.

'Go to the circle where you must hold hands, dance around singing 'Here We Go Round The Mulberry Bush'; see what happens,' said the foolish aunt.

Ben winced at the idea.

The two fruit-stained children followed their dotty aunt's strange orders. As they sang the last words they found themselves standing under the mulberry tree, sheltering from the rain, Ben holding the pot-bellied pig's lead as before. The children looked at each other in surprise and bewilderment.

'How did the old bat do that?' said Ben.

'I don't like this weird place.' Lucy shivered as they walked towards their aunt's home, where they found nothing amiss.

Ignoring the children she welcomed Porodos like a lost child, dried his body with a soft, peach-coloured towel then placed him in a fur-lined dog basket, not forgetting his pink, fluffy, covered hot water bottle. Both children questioned the old lady about Mulberry Land. She denied everything, yet it was the same person, the mole and three ginger hairs were there, no mistaking them.

'You have such strange imaginations,' she said smiling. 'What a silly story to invent, are you both mad, or were you struck by lightning? Off to bed with you, a sleep will do you good.'

'I'm hungry, I want something to eat,' sighed Ben. 'A bacon sarnie would do.'

Porodos squirmed uncomfortably in his bed.

'We never have bacon in this house,' said Aunt Dottie, 'it upsets my little darling. Off you go.' The mole hairs twitched in anger.

Two hungry, perplexed children went to bed.

'I'm right pleased we are going home tomorrow,' said Ben.

'Me too, I never want to come to this sad place again,' wailed Lucy.

That evening, several lorries arrived at Aunt Dottie's gate. The two children watch from their window, the drivers were ordered to deliver their loads to Farmer Quibble's pig field.

'Share it well,' Auntie told them.

'What's the weird old bat up to now?' asked Ben.

'Beats me,' said Lucy as she crawled into bed.

Next morning, as soon as their taxi arrived, Ben and Lucy rushed to get away, waving briefly to their strange aunt. No way would they kiss her and the hairy mole goodbye. She smiled sweetly as the taxi drove away.

'Good riddance,' she said under her breath. 'They won't come back in a hurry darling Porodos. Have another jelly baby, my beautiful.'

As the taxi passed Farmer Quibble's field, a strange sight met their eyes. Through the early morning mist, they saw pigs floating and drifting, some struggling on the ground hoping for lift off. The air was full of strange smells, pigs rose upward, jet propelled by hot curry gas; loud smelly raspberries spurted from the rear ends of the squealing pigs. Some of them made it over the hedge; they were free and ran for their lives. Low flying pigs collided in mid-air. Farmer Quibble chased every which way to catch the gas-filled porkers, pandemonium had broken loose; so had the wind in the pigs. Some squiggled and spluttered in the air like party balloons, ending their flight dangling in trees and hedges. The taxi driver stared at the hilarious sight. 'They say pigs might fly, I've actually seen them do it now! Are they filming a TV comedy over there?' he asked.

Ben and Lucy fell back in their seats laughing and squealing like pigs, holding their noses. 'Pooh, what a stink,' Ben giggled, 'Auntie must have tried the mixture, and it's worked.'

'That was the weirdest weekend I've ever had,' Lucy laughed as the flying pig circus faded from view. With a twinkle in her eye she said, 'Perhaps one day we will go back to see Aunt Dottie, Ben.'

'And pigs might fly,' he chuckled!

MAGGIE AND THE SNAKE

Ann-Marie Spittle

Maggie is a ginger cat with one eye, but as with all cats, Maggie still thinks she is the most beautiful cat in the world and Ethan, the little boy who owns her, agrees.

Maggie knew the day was going to be strange because Ethan was ready for school before his mother had to ask him to get ready, or even before she had made his packed lunch. He had also brushed his teeth, brushed his hair, and got his shoes on before she needed to ask him. His friend Robert arrived early, and was talking nineteen to the dozen about an escaped snake, and how their school may have to be shut down. The snake was last seen near the school grounds.

Ethan's mother was very worried and called the school. The headmaster told her there was nothing to worry about and that the children would be very safe on the school premises, as a special snake catcher had been in the school and said it was safe for the children to attend classes.

Ethan walked to school wondering if a giant snake, or even a crocodile, would leap out of the bushes along the path to school and eat his friend as they walked down the road. Now that would be something to write about in English that day!

Maggie watched him go and wondered why everyone was so excited. She heard Ethan's auntie talking about getting her machete out of the wardrobe 'In case 'it' got into their house,' she said. (A machete is a very large-bladed knife that people use in the jungle to cut plants out of their way so they can walk through it easier. Ethan's auntie had been working out in Africa when she'd got the machete, and kept it locked in her wardrobe. 'Just in case,' she said.)

Out in the grass of next door's garden, a rat was sat in the grass sunning himself, eating a piece of old biscuit and wondering, *what is that awful smell?* What he didn't know was that he wasn't going to see another sunny day, because a very large snake was looking at him from the grass, and was thinking of having him for dinner!

The snake moved slowly through the grass. Not a blade was disturbed as it slowly slid along the ground, leaving a large path between the blades of grass as if a bicycle had been wheeled through it. The rat scratched its ears, looked around to see if it could find some seeds hanging from the blades of grass, leant forward to take a seed, and the snake struck! The rat didn't even have time to let out a squeak as the snake crushed the life out of it and slowly started to swallow the rat, making itself look like an onion stuck in a sock, but Sparkle, the magpie knew what was really in the lump.

Back in the house, Maggie was sunning herself as usual on the window sill. If she knew what was undulating its way around next door's garden, she would have been a white cat.

Ethan's mother left for work and all was quiet in the house.

Maggie heard Sparkle squawking. He was trying to tell Maggie that the snake was in her garden, but Maggie was taking no notice. 'Stupid bird. What is it complaining about now?' and fell asleep.

It started off as a small squawk then got louder, and louder, making Maggie turn towards the window and shake her paw at him. 'Shut up will you. You're really starting to hurt my head. *Shut up!*' she shouted.

Sparkle pointed at the grass with his wings, but Maggie thought he was making a fuss because Ethan's mum hadn't left any food out for him.

'Oh do get lost you stupid flying fleabag, you're really going to get it in a minute!' she turned away again.

The snake was getting closer to the house. Maggie couldn't see it because her good eye was underneath the edge of the window frame. If she had, she'd have been a couple of pounds smaller because of the size of that thing.

It was the smell that made her sit up. It made her think of rotting meat. She looked out of the window and saw the biggest mouth she had ever seen. 'Aarghhh!' she screamed, then pulled her claws out of the ceiling and jumped back onto the window sill. The snake was nowhere to be seen. *Thank God Ethan's mum shuts the windows before she goes out*, thought Maggie, or she'd be another lump in the snake by now.

Little did Maggie know, but the snake was hiding under the window waiting for her to come and have a look. The snake knew that cats, especially Maggie-type cats, were extremely nosy and couldn't pass up the chance to have a good nose. Often with really bad consequences.

She walked around the house, and noticed that Ethan's mother had left the window open in the bathroom again. Always a good way to get out into the garden, and even better if you want to get back into the house before anyone notices you weren't in the house. So she jumped onto the side of the bath, leapt onto the window sill and jumped out of the bathroom window. She landed on the roof of the kitchen lean-to, climbed onto the drainpipe and slid down it, using her claws to grip the pipe.

The snake had heard her jumping around in the house, the scrape of her nails on the pipe, and was waiting around the corner for her with its mouth open.

She jumped up onto the wall and the snake hit its head on it trying to get at her.

'Damn,' said the snake.

Maggie walked along the wall, but because the snake was on her bad eye side, she didn't see it. So the snake followed by keeping to the edge of the wall, well out of her view.

Sparkle was still shouting at Maggie as she walked along the wall. She sat at the end and told him to shut up. He was getting annoying now.

The snake got closer and reared up so it could get a good strike at Maggie, but as it went forward, Maggie moved towards Sparkle, threatening to kill him if he didn't stop squawking. 'Don't you know there's a snake in the garden?' She cried.

The snake tried again, and just missed getting a bite of Maggie's tail. Sparkle was nearly having a heart attack. How could he get Maggie to move to where he was on the roof, and stop the snake from eating her?

Just then, the rat from next door, who spoke cat, jumped up to talk to Maggie, saw the snake, said, 'Oh my gosh, a snake!' and ran off.

Maggie turned, saw the snake, jumped off the wall, ran through the grass and got tangled in Ethan's bicycle. The snake slowly slinked towards Maggie with a smug look on its face. Maggie struggled even more, but the chain came off Ethan's bike and held her down. The snake got hold of Maggie's tail and started to swallow it. She miaowed really loudly. The snake swallowed some more, she miaowed again.

Just as she thought the snake was going to start to swallow her legs, a very large sword chopped the snake's head off, and part of Maggie's tail with it. 'Reowwwww,' she screamed.

Ethan's auntie had come home early for lunch, seen the snake following Maggie along the wall, got her machete out of her wardrobe, come down and chopped its head off just in time.

She took Maggie to the vet and had the part of the tail from in the snake sewn back on, had a big bandage put on the end of her tail, and taken her home.

When Ethan came home and saw Maggie's tail and found out what had happened, he started to cry because Maggie could have been snake food if his auntie hadn't saved her. He gave Maggie and his auntie a big hug and kiss.

Ethan's mum called the police and got them to take the snake away, but not before Ethan and his friends had their picture taken with the dead snake's head. His mum scrubbed him like mad with Tea Tree soap when she caught him, and told him off about picking up dead things that were covered in germs. You could hear the screams down the street.

Weeks later, Maggie's bandage came off and the hair on the end had gone completely white.

'Because of the shock,' the vet said.

So now when Maggie walks around in the dark, you can see one glowing green eye and a glowing white tip.

But Ethan still loves her.

B.E

J Wildon

Just as Polly-Wink and Bunty were sitting down to a cup of their favourite lemon-leaf tea, a knock came at the door.

'Now, who can that be?' Polly-Wink looked over the top of her glasses at Bunty.

Bunty shook her head. 'I don't know. Do you think we ought to answer it?'

'Well, if we don't, we'll never know who it is!' and Polly-Wink walked briskly over to the door.

On the step outside stood Mr McRabb, the delivery man.

'Parcel for you, Miss Polly-Wink,' he said. 'Please sign here.'

Polly-Wink took his book and wrote her name next to where he was pointing.

'Shall I carry it in for you,' asked Mr McRabb, 'it *is* rather heavy?' And he picked it up and put it in the middle of the sitting-room floor. 'Well, then, I'll be off. Good day, ladies,' and away he went again.

Polly-Wink and Bunty walked round and round the large brown paper parcel.

'Whatever can it be?' asked Bunty. 'It can't be a birthday present as you had a birthday two months ago, and Christmas and Easter are a long way off.'

'Well, it's certainly addressed to me,' said Polly-Wink, taking a closer look at the label, 'so we'd better open it and see.'

The two of them soon had the paper off, and were tearing away excitedly at the brown cardboard box.

'Goodness gracious me! An elephant!' exclaimed Polly-Wink, stepping hastily backwards.

'It's only a . . . *baby* elephant,' whispered Bunty, peering out from behind the settee.

'But why, and *who* would send me an elephant, baby or otherwise?' asked Polly-Wink of nobody in particular.

'Perhaps there is a card or something in with it?' suggested Bunty, coming out from behind the settee, and sure enough there was.

'Dear Polly-Wink,' it said, 'I picked this up at a car boot sale and thought you might find a use for it. Love, Great-Aunt Mabel.'

'A *use* for it! What use would I have for an elephant! It'll just have to go back to Great-Aunt Mabel!'

'Please - please, don't send me back,' a tiny voice said.

'Oh,' Polly-Wink bent her head and stared down at the little elephant. 'And, *why* not, may I ask?'

'Because I was so unhap . . . hap . . . happy before,' and a large tear dropped from his little eye and travelled all the way down his little trunk, to fall with a plop onto the carpet. Another one swiftly followed, to Polly-Wink's alarm.

'Oh, *do* stop crying, you'll flood the room!' she said.

So the little elephant tried hard to stop, and just gavc onc or two sniffs in his trunk and let his whole body droop pathetically.

'What do you think we should do, Polly-Wink?' asked Bunty.

'Well, I don't really see how we can send him back. Great Aunt would be most hurt, even offended, which could be worse. And what would *she* do with him? No, we'll just have to keep it! What's your name?' she asked the little elephant.

He shook his head sadly. 'I've never had one,' he replied.

'Well, we'll have to call you *something*.' Polly-Wink put her head on one side. 'Any ideas Bunty?'

Bunty thought for a minute. 'What about - Baby Elephant?' she suggested.

'Baby Elephant? B.E for short? Yes, that will do,' Polly-Wink nodded. 'But as to *usefulness* - what can he do?'

But it soon became clear B.E had a lot of uses. He could put his little trunk right under the beds and suck up all the fluff - a job that Polly-Wink and Bunty had been unable to do themselves. He could also water the garden from the water-butt, standing there squirting water around in all directions. They found he could reach up with his trunk and neatly pick apples from the trees, putting them down carefully into a basket at his feet. They taught him to walk along a row of lettuces, or flowers, with two legs on either side of the row, pulling up the weeds and popping them into a bin strapped to his back, and when the leaves fell from the trees, he 'hoovered' them up.

They even bought themselves a hammock and slung it between two trees, and B.E would push it gently backwards and forwards with them inside! Oh, he was making himself useful in so many ways that they couldn't imagine how they had managed without him.

One day, Polly-Wink and Bunty were busy in their garden, whilst B.E sat on the edge of the little pool sucking up water in his trunk, then squirting it out again, aiming at the many little fish who were swimming about. Once he sucked up one by mistake, and on squirting it back into the water again, he had received a *very* black look from it, and a 'Do you mind!'

Polly-Wink put down her trowel. 'Bunty,' she said turning to her friend, 'I am getting rather worried about B.E. He has been with us a long time now, and I think we ought to think what we should do with him now he is getting bigger.'

'What do you mean, Polly-Wink?' Bunty sat back on her heels to look at Polly-Wink.

'Well,' said Polly-Wink, 'he's *not* B.E anymore, is he? He's getting quite big.'

Bunty laughed. 'Well, if that's all that is troubling you, we can still call him B.E, only the B would stand for *big* instead of *baby*!'

'No, Bunty, it's not that, but he takes up so much room now. I mean, we cannot get close to the fire when it is cold, because he lays down in front of it and pushes us out. And if he turns round, everything gets upset. And when he sneezes . . . Oh, I could go on and on. But apart from that, he is beginning to get bored.'

'Yes, I know he is,' replied Bunty. 'I notice that when he picks apples these days, he is starting to *eat* them, just for something to do. But, we cannot just tell him to leave, can we? We're much too fond of him.'

'No, of course we can't. But I thought, perhaps, we might be able to find him a job,' Polly-Wink tried to sound hopeful.

'Such as spraying crops on a farm, or with the local fire brigade, putting out fires,' sarcastically suggested Bunty.

'No.' Polly-Wink sounded annoyed. 'We could put an advert in the paper, see what replies we get.'

'Well, let's see what B.E thinks. He might not like the idea.'

So they called B.E over, and sat in a circle on the grass.

'B.E we've been thinking,' Polly-Wink began nervously, 'now you have grown so big, we are going to call you *Big* Elephant instead of *Baby* B.E still, of course, what do you think?'

B.E looked pleased and waggled his head in agreement.

'And as you are so big now, you must see a little more of life outside of here. Of course, still live here, but get something more *interesting* to do to fill your day.'

'But I'm perfectly happy here, Aunt Polly-Wink,' B.E sounded puzzled.

'Yes, I know,' Polly-Wink tried to sound calm although she was not, 'but you don't want to grow up and have people call you "Dumbo-Jumbo" now do you?'

B.E shook his head.

'So,' continued Polly-Wink, 'we thought an advert in the paper for a job. Something like, "Smart, intelligent elephant seeks suitable job. Any offer considered."'

B.E sat up a little straighter. Smart, intelligent? Well, yes, he supposed he was.

The offers of jobs surprised them. From walking over the greens of a bowling club - because their roller had broken down - with a small salary, plus free cakes and buns on match days, to walking across someone's garden, making footprints to be filled in with concrete to form an unusual path. And so it went on.

The one offering free buns was the deciding factor, and B.E arrived in good time, to find no one about. But he decided to start on the task anyway, walking and running up and down over the immaculate bowling greens. Somehow or other, the greens did not appear to be immaculate now after he had worked so hard on them, and he sat down to rest in one of the little seats beside the area, only to feel it give way under him and send him sprawling. After trying two more, with the same thing happening, he got up and ambled away; passing the club house, he saw rows of buns on a table inside. Ah! That must be for him! So in and out snaked his long trunk, until not one bun was left. Contentedly, he laid down under the window - yes, he decided, this was the job he liked!

Suddenly he heard voices coming from the room.

'Joan,' said voice number one. 'I thought you were doing the teas today?'

'Yes I am. Why?' That was voice number two.

'Well, you'd better get on with it, the players will soon be here.'

Voice number two sounded smug. 'If you look, you will see that I have already done so.'

Voice number one, 'Must be invisible, then.'

Silence. Then voice number two, 'But I did, Valerie, I did!'

Voice number one, 'It's those boys from the school again! Come on, we'll go over and see the headmaster.'

B.E had a sudden suspicion that those particular buns were not part of his payment - so he got up quickly and trotted back home.

Bunty was in the kitchen when he arrived. 'I thought you'd be starving after your first day,' she said, 'so I've made you a very, very big apple pie, all to yourself.'

Poor B.E was so full of buns that he could not bring himself to have even the *smallest* piece of pie. He just laid down and went to sleep.

'Perhaps they worked him too hard,' said a worried Polly-Wink, 'and he is just exhausted. I don't think we will let him go tomorrow, Bunty, it'll be too much for him.'

And as for the bowling club, they never found out what had happened to their buns, or who had spoilt their immaculate bowling green!

OSWALD AND THE BROKEN BOOT

Ray Smart

It was dark in the garden, very dark. In fact Oswald the Viking had never known it as dark before, and it worried him.

During the day he was a little stone figure who couldn't even move without being carried or pushed or pulled by someone, but when the clock struck twelve, if there were no people around, and if there was just a little glow of light, Oswald could move. The brighter the light became, the faster he could walk or run. Sometimes if the light shone really brightly, he could even jump.

Tonight it was ever so dark, and Oswald was concerned. He couldn't see very well and couldn't move at all, yet he had an awful lot to do. Tonight he really needed to get around the garden quickly. He thought about things!

The main problem concerned Eddy, the little bear fisherman. He'd had an accident during the day - well not exactly an accident. The dog that lived in the big house had attacked him - well not Eddy really, his fishing rod. It had broken the rod and chewed the old boot that Eddy had caught on his hook. So poor Eddy was left just sitting by the little pool with his arms stretched out and his hands clasped together, but there was nothing to hold in them. He was very upset. Oswald knew that because he could see Eddy crying. He could also see the boot and the rod. They were lying in the middle of the driveway in a quite dangerous place. He shouted to Eddy, 'Don't worry Eddy, I'm coming to help you!' But Eddy just sat there looking sad, staring straight in front of him. He shouted even louder, as loud as he could, 'Cheer up, I'm on my way to help you!' But either the little bear was too upset to answer, or he just could not hear. 'Poor Eddy, he's getting more and more unhappy,' Oswald said to himself.

It was still quite dark and he could hardly move, so Oswald looked around the garden. The little pot owl on the rockery just stared straight past him, not even blinking his eye - there'd be no use asking him for help. What about the flower sellers? There were two of them, one quite close to where the attack had happened, the other was nearer to Oswald in the garden. He had quite an unusual name. Something like Lissi or Lizzie. Oswald scratched his head trying to remember. Then it came to him - Lycidas -yes that was it! A strange name for a boy, but he was a strange kind of person. He just stood there, near the fishpond, looking at his flowers, well staring at them really but not even trying to sell them. Oswald didn't think that he would want to help. The other flower seller was a little girl who had only recently come into the garden. Oswald had not spoken to her before, so he did not know her name. She looked nice, with her pretty green hat and her beautiful flowers. *Perhaps she'll help,* he thought, *I'll shout to her and ask.*

'*Yoo-hoo,*' called Oswald. There was no answer from the girl. He cupped his hands around his lips. '*Yoo-hoo,* flower girl, can you hear me?' Oswald thought she looked as though she might have heard him but she didn't answer.

He called again, this time so loud that if he had been able to move very much, he would probably have fallen off the big square stone on which he was sitting. Just then, something quite wonderful happened. The little girl smiled at him and held up her flower basket. The smile sort of lit up her face - and the basket, in fact it seemed to make everything in the garden brighter and then, when he smiled back, Oswald felt himself becoming lighter and stronger, then, quite suddenly, he could move properly.

Down from the stone he dropped, hurrying while there was still some light from the smiles, over to the drive where he quickly picked up the rod, which luckily hadn't been broken, and the boot, which had been broken, but only a little. Oswald didn't think that would matter too much, as he could still tie it back on to the fishing line. He soon did this and went to where Eddy was sitting and put the rod and line back into his hands. Eddy didn't say anything, but Oswald thought that he probably couldn't move much because the light of the smiles hadn't quite reached him, though he was sure Eddy looked happier.

As Oswald hurried back to his stone, just managing to climb back onto it before his strength went, he was glad he had managed to solve another problem in the garden.

Arbo The Bear

Maureen Rhodes

Once upon a time, not so long ago, lived a little boy named Edwards. His father was very rich and so Edward had an enormous amount of toys to play with.

One morning as his mother was cleaning the house, she happened to stumble over some of the toys. Picking them up she took them straight to Edward's room. 'But this room is packed with so many toys it's a wonder Edward can find his bed at night,' she gasped as she closed the door gently. On Edward's return from school, she explained to him that he had to do something about all the toys in his room.

That night, Edward and his mother sat down just before bed and talked about the best thing to do.

Many suggestions were made, but finally, Edward decided that he might like to give some of them away to a charity shop. The very next morning, Edward and his father placed some toys into a big brown box and set out in the car to the charity shop.

The lady in the shop was delighted, 'Toys are not something we get every day, so many children do not like parting with them.'

Edward looked at his father, as he knew that he also had loved his toys, but knew he had many more at home.

'It just goes to show,' said the lady, 'you must be a very special boy indeed.'

This made Edward feel very proud and he walked out of the shop with a huge smile on his face.

That evening, before closing, the lady began to sort through the box, placing each toy carefully on the shelves. At the very bottom of the box she found a droopy little teddy bear, which was so very floppy and ragged, that she placed him on the top shelf. This took many attempts, as the bear did not sit very easily. The bear now sat in the far corner, where it was very dark, which made the bear extremely unhappy and very sad indeed. All that the little bear wanted was to be loved and cared for, and now because he could not be seen, this would never happen. One by one all the other toys disappeared from the shelves, and he began to believe that nobody wanted this poor, shabby and unlovable bear.

The little bear did not realise, that in the same road, lived a little boy named Billy, who in many ways was just like the bear. Billy was not sad, in fact he was a very brave and happy little boy, but Billy actually could not walk. Billy got around by way of a wheelchair, which was painted in very bright colours. He had a windmill fitted to it, which would spin around as he went along. Billy was always cheerful and therefore had many friends, his happiness shone to all around him.

One fine day, his mother was pushing him down the street, when she stopped to look in the window of the charity shop. Billy noticed the tiny bear up on the top shelf in the corner. The bear was all bent up and looked very sad and dusty.

'Mum,' Billy cried out, 'you have to take me in this shop, I must find out about that bear.'

He was wheeled in, by his mother and taken straight to the counter, where he asked if he could buy the bear. His mother noticed that Billy looked rather sad, which was not like him at all.

'I'm sorry,' said the shop assistant, 'I can't sell you that bear,' at which Billy lowered his head. 'But I can give him to you, only because I know he will be loved and looked after,' she announced quite boldly.

Billy's face lit up once again and within seconds the little bear was in his arms receiving lots of cuddles and of course, love.

When they arrived home, the bear and Billy sat for hours just staring at each other. That night when Billy's father came home, Billy explained how he had got the bear. Father looked at the teddy for a long while and then turning to Billy announced, 'Well son, he is disabled just like you are, so maybe let's see what we can do to help him, shall we?'

Father got out his big box of tools from the shed and made a splint to support the teddy's back, so that he would be able to sit up by himself. Next he made the teddy a wheelchair and painted it exactly the same as Billy's chair, he even placed a windmill on the top.

The very next day when all the work was finished, Billy noticed that the bear was smiling and looking extremely happy. Billy and his new friend went everywhere together; he even went with Billy to the hospital when he had to have his own treatment. As they were sitting in the waiting room, Billy realised that his bear did not have a name.

Billy sat and thought for a long while. Suddenly Billy shouted out, 'Mr Arbo, that's your name.' And from that day till this, his new friend is known as Arbo the bear, and as far as I know Billy and Arbo are living very happy and cheerful lives together, despite their disabilities. Billy found a toy that he could identify with and Arbo found the love and care that he had always longed for. And so, for two very special young people a new friendship was started. Which goes to show that even though sometimes we may be different on the outside, on the inside we are all the same.

SEAFLOATERS

Stella Robinson

It's the year 3000 - looking out onto the horizon, the sun is going down. There are no people on this land, in this life. There's a big ocean; glistening, like stars caught in the peaks of the sea. There are huge snowy mountains that go on for miles. There is no country or shops. The only land creatures are eagles, crocs and dinosaurs. Every few yards there are whirlpools of heated water, with steam billowing out of them. It's a hostile but beautiful fairyland.

Mankind - existence of people - all died out about a thousand years ago, when all of a sudden a volcano erupted and all the people all over the world turned to stone (the terror must have been unimaginable). This world seemed so lonely, the vast cavity of sea spilling on for eternity.

An eagle croc flying above (which is like a dinosaur bird); quite big, with a yellow and green body and wings; croaking desperately, trying to skim shrimp from the surface of the sea - ducking and diving - swoosh! He caught some. He's happy as can be.

A big splash of tornados - out of the sea two mermaids came whizzing from the deep; Tatiana and Centuri came to investigate. Tatiana had a half-human body (at the top) and a light pink fishtail (on the bottom), she had huge, round green eyes and blonde curly hair that went on forever. Centuri had a light blue fishtail, blue hair and yellow eyes. They were young sweethearts (both aged 17); ducking and diving and playing fish-tag (a game of 'tag', in other words). They were really happy; giggling like little children. They didn't come to the surface much in case a dinosaur saw them and came off-land to get them. Tatiana was bubbly and playful and Centuri was more serious, but loving.

It was time they went down to the deepest depths of the sea; back to their homes. So they bolted together; like bullets, gliding through the sea. Along the way was a huge, pretty, yellow sea horse – she was holding a huge sea-shell (lit with twinkling lights) for Tatiana and Centuri to take. It was a special gift (because they were both due to turn 18), a gift from King Nemesis (the ruler of the mermaid kingdom); a blue-finned and silver-haired mermaid; a granddad to everyone. King

Nemesis was like a crab; hard on the outside and soft on the inside - he liked everyone to keep the rules.

Eventually, Tatiana and Centuri got extremely deep, where the pressure was strong and bubbles and shrimps galore were all around. Tatiana held on tightly to Centuri's back and they belted through the most dangerous chamber, arriving home in the land of Starfin. There were hundreds of seafloaters (ie, mermaids) all around; young and old, middle-aged, it was like rainbows darting everywhere. Everyone had their own castle. Tatiana and Centuri had a gold castle, with open cavities, glittering with glitter and dripping pearls, hanging like ornaments. In the middle was a huge gold four poster bed, a gold bedside lamp on a mother-of-pearl table and white books with shells encrusted upon them - rainbow lights cascaded all around the hollow walls.

If they wanted, the seafloaters could join in activities (like races) with the other seafloaters, or race on huge colourful sea horses. Sea horses were the favourites; they would smile and talk telepathically. Also, they could visit the fish-prisons where monsters were caught and where naughty mermaids were kept. They could also have an educational lesson with King Nemesis on 'sea life and discipline'.

Anyway, Tatiana and Centuri are floating together (anxiously) in a corner, hesitating to open the seashell - then Tatiana pings open the shell - in the middle is a key; a small gold glittering key with a small note. It says, 'Take the key to the middle chamber at door number eighteen, then enter, to the journey of your life!' They swam for a while and arrived at door number eighteen. They opened the door and there was a magical party going on, but it wasn't their clan of mermaids; it was human people, pretty women in colourful satin dresses (blues, pinks, yellows, reds, etc, etc) with ruffles and frills coming out like bells, their hair pinned up with curls coming down. Also, men in black suits and white shirts (very handsome men). Some were dancing together to pretty music called 'The Great Waltz', others were sitting on red velvet chairs; talking, smoking and laughing. There were sparkling 'chandeliers' dripping down, and rich red carpets and gold walls everywhere. There was also food: chicken, cheese, grapes and potatoes.

Tatiana and Centuri couldn't believe their eyes. Tatiana became all emotional and started crying.

'What can this be?' Centuri said.

'It's not our world, but it's a heavenly world,' Tatiana said.

They mingled around the Victorian people in a trance and reached out to touch them, but there was no feeling; they were like ghosts. Tatiana and Centuri started dancing around them, they couldn't believe their luck; they were so happy. At the end of the room was another door which led to another room. They went into room 19 - the door slowly creaked open and they were in a big castle with grey stone brick walls, with huge paintings on the walls of ladies in green floaty dresses of velvet and men were in velvet trousers (in many colours) up to the knees, and pointy shoes.

A middle-aged lady with a stern face was sitting at a desk. It was Queen Victoria, with ginger hair tied into a severe bun. Her dress had black and silver checks all over it, billowing out beneath her. She was demanding for a letter to be written to the Government by a servant man. A few sips of red wine and she began dictating. Tatiana and Centuri were amazed, they said they thought this world was a strict world. They found it fascinating, but they were glad they were not in this world.

Eventually they left out of a big red exit door and a gush of water pulled them along for about a mile. Then they arrived home. Tatiana and Centuri were very thankful to their master, King Nemesis, for giving them this magical coming-of-age gift. It was a dream they will never forget.

Magic Moments

Wendy Watkin

'Well George, I don't think we'll have any problems with this, it's not messy or anything, should keep him out of mischief.'

'Yes, hope you're right dear.'

'Oh, here he is now, many happy returns, Neil, come on, have a look what we've got you, should keep you occupied.'

Off came the cheerful wrapping paper to reveal - 'A Magician's Box of Tricks.'

Neil's face dropped. *What do they think I'm gonna do with that?* he thought.

'Cor, great! Thanks Mum, Dad,' he said, trying to sound reasonably grateful . . .

'Here you are, Son, but be careful, we don't want any mishaps.'

'Roller skates! Cor, just what I wanted, Uncle Dick, thanks a bunch!'

'I'm not very enthusiastic about Dick's present, George, but - still - boys will be boys, I suppose, I just hope he's careful.'

'Don't worry dear, you can't wrap them up in cotton wool forever, can you?'

Neil carried the presents up to his bedroom, and decided he may as well inspect the magic set. There may be something of interest in it!

He rummaged around, and found a few colourful objects, some instructions and some sort of 'magic mirror'.

Dunno what that's for, he thought, shoving it to one side, then picking it up again, he noticed it was sticky on one side, made of paper. he unrolled it, and stuck it on the wall. Not quite knowing what to do, he tired of it, and glanced down at the shiny roller skates. They seemed more interesting, he'd try them out. He picked them up and put them on; then stood admiring himself in that magic mirror.

Taking a few steps backwards, he started skating in front of the mirror . . . then - all of a sudden - the mirror appeared to get closer, and closer, and bigger and *zoom!* he went straight through it, *whoosh!* as he went, he saw a long lane, covered in gold . . .

He picked himself up, and noticed castles on either side, and then - a 'wizard-like being'.

'Who are you?' he said, wonderingly, 'and where am I?'

'I'm Mr Grant A Great Wish, and this is the lane of 'longings and dreams', where all that you wish, is not what it seems.'

Don't know that I like the sound of that, he thought . . .

Further along the lane were a few more people. 'What are they doing here?' he said.

'They're waiting for me to grant their wishes,' said the wizard, 'you may even know them . . .'

Neil wondered along the lane and spotted a familiar face. 'Oh no, not Mr Frogalfic, not old frog-face, of all people, I can't be doing with him, I see enough of him at school.'

'Neil, my boy, so nice to see you, in this land of longings, perhaps we can learn something useful, here,' he said.

'B-but I don't know how I got here, or if I even like it,' said Neil.

'Oh you will, you will, my boy, wait and see!'

Then on closer inspection he saw two very familiar faces, coming toward him.

'I say, Tommy, it's Neil!'

'By jove, so it is, Charlie!'

'Neil, old chap, we didn't expect to see you here. How did you get here?'

'Dunno, really, something to do with a mirror.'

'A mirror! What do you mean?'

'Well, I-I sort of, sort of - slid through it.'

'Blimy,' said Charlie!'

'What about you two?' said Neil.

'Wi don't know, wi were huntin' conkers, and crawled through some brambles and ended up here,' said Tommy.

'Cor! and guess who's over there, 'Frogface'.'

'Huh! that's all we need, see enough of his ugly mug at school,' said Charlie.

'What'll we do, then; is there a way out, do you think?' said Neil.

'But wiv bin promised anythin wi want, I've bin offered as much cake as I can eat, an' I'm starvin'!' said Tommy.

'Oh you would, you always are,' said Neil.

'Well wouldn't you want the pick of anything, old chap, if it's offered to you on a plate. I may select the biggest chocolate Easter egg,' said Charlie.

'S-spose so, I do like cake, I could eat it forever!' said Neil, excitedly.

'Well, then, let's hang around, then, and wait our turn,' said Charlie eagerly.

'But it'll take ages, look at the queue!' said Neil, impatiently.

'Eee - ya right, lad, we're nowhere near front, we'll get nowt for hours,' said Tommy.

'Well I say we explore, come on!' said Charlie.

'Look at all em exquisite castles! What do ya think's in 'em?' said Tommy.

'Dunno,' said Neil, 'but we could soon find out . . .'

'Don't go in there, don't go in there, for goodness sake!' said a funny, flabby, wobbly sort of being.'

'Why not?' said Charlie, 'and who are you, anyway?'

'I'm Mr Flibble-de-gib, and I tell you it's not safe.'

'Int it,' said Tommy, 'why?'

'Well, all this business about wishes and things, well - it be a right load of trollop - rubbish, that what it be, and, you be well to keep clear of it. All they want to do is feed ee up, and then' - he snapped his fingers . . .

'Then, what?' said Charlie, shaking in his boots.

'Then - hey presto! You're a toad, or a frog, or some other unimaginable creature they wish to turn ee into, and I know cos I've seen it 'appen'.'

'Crikey!' said Charlie.

'Flippin' ek!' said Tommy.

'Oh take no notice of him, he's pulling our legs, he's just trying to hog all the goodies to himself,' said Neil.

'I'm not, I tell ee, if you go in there, you'll be dead meat, and that's for sure.'

'Oh shurrup!' said Tommy, 'I'm going back down lane.'

'Well wait for us, we're coming, aren't we, Neil?'

Then - all of a sudden - a dozen ugly gremlins appeared from behind the trees. Running, chanting - and chasing the three boys, down the lane.

'Higgle-de piggle-de, higgle-de-piggles! We're gonna get you, we're the fliggles!'

'Oh no!' said Neil, 'oh no!'

'Come on, come on, quick, run!'

'Steady on - steady on! Calm down!' said a friendly voice.

'Uncle Dick, I'm so pleased to see you, but I didn't know you knew where we were,' said Neil, panting breathlessly.

'I was contacted by the mayor of the mirror, and told of the danger you could be in, if you succumbed to any of these deadly wishes.'

'Do you know what we can do, then,' said Charlie.

'Aye - hurry up, then,' said Tommy, 'look, they're catching up, quick!'

'Well, for a start, we've to get back to that mirror of yours, Neil, and you, have to get back through it.'

'B-but how?'

'Same way you got in, put those skates on, knew I did the wrong thing giving you those, but still - you learn by your mistakes, don't you?'

'I were lookin' forward to that cake I were goin' to wish for, spose it's out of the question now,' said Tommy, sadly.

'Ah well,' said Uncle Dick, 'there's bad cake, and good cake, and this is what we're aiming for, to eat the good cake. That will bring us the magical power to beckon the mayor of the mirror, to whoosh us back through. So come on, we must rush, as quickly as we can, grab the good cake, wish, and before you know it, we'll be back, all safe and well.'

'What about Frogalfic, do we tell him?'

'Oh dunno, can we leave him here?' said Neil.

'Oh come on now, he is one of us, you know,' said Uncle Dick.

'Aye, we'll atta let 'im come, it's only fair,' said Tommy.

'Yeah, spose so,' said Neil, as they all ran hell for leather, down the golden lane to where the wishes were granted.

'How will we know if it's the right, I mean - good cake?' said Charlie.

'Look for the cherry, it must have a cherry on it, then you'll know,' said Uncle Dick.

'Eee - champion! Oh, oh, they're comin'!' said Tommy.

'Higgle-de-piggle, higgle-di-pum, we're the fliggles, you'd better run!'

'Oh no, quick!' said Neil, 'quick!'

Tommy flopped carelessly to the ground, exhausted.

‘Get up, get up, Tommy, there’s no time to loll,’ said Charlie.

‘Oh - phew! there’s Mr Grant A Great Wish, waiting for us, come on!’ said Neil, hurrying at great speed.

‘Right, now - don’t forget, don’t forget the cherry, we must eat the right cake,’ said Uncle Dick . . .

Neil took hold of the large piece of cake, and slowly eased it toward his open mouth . . .

Uncle Dick’s face dropped in fright, ‘Oh no! Oh no, don’t!’

Neil started to go dizzy, and woozy, his head was spinning, he let out a yell, as he was about to take a bite of the cake.

‘No! It’s the wrong cake, Neil, no, don’t eat it!’ But it was too late, it had slithered down in one go, and Neil was spluttering and coughing, suddenly . . .

‘Neil, you’re going to be alright, I’m here, your dad’s here, you gave us a nasty shock crashing through that mirror with those skates on.

Neil came to his senses and looked up to see his mum, and dad, looking down at him.

‘W-w-where am I - oh, is this hospital? Ooh, now I remember!’

‘Yes, and I hope you remember to be more careful in future, those flippin’ skates, Dick should never have brought them, anyway, it’s just concussion, we’ll have you out of here in no time. You don’t want to miss your party, do you? The cake’s all ready and waiting.’

‘Oh Mum! Could we give the cake a miss, do you think?’

The Ship's Cat

H W Spicer

A retired ship's cat called Nelson padded around the corner, into a street in the old quarter of Liverpool Docklands. Halfway down, he stops at a ramshackle warehouse bearing a weathered and fading sign 'Flynn's Ship Chandlers'. He enters through the archway into an enclosed yard, with storerooms, offices and living accommodation leading off. It no longer functions as a ship chandlery, but Ma Flynn, who still lives on the premises, hires the offices and store rooms to a local wine merchant. She's a pert, lively seventy year old and drives a hard bargain when it comes to fixing the rent. Her husband died several years ago. Some said it broke his heart when so many of the great transatlantic liners disappeared from the Liverpool scene and his ship stores were no longer required.

Nelson made his way to Ma Flynn's outer office, the central feature of which is an old fashioned coal-burning stove, and around it, several fellow-cats are perched, yarning about old times. They include, currently serving ships' cats on leave, unemployed ships' cats waiting for an opportunity to go back to sea and would-be ships' cats looking for a maiden voyage. There are also a few retired, over-the-hill sea-cats like himself who still need that contact with the old days. Saucers of milk and plates of sardines are placed strategically around the room. He moved over to a tortoise-shell tom called Kipper, named after his favourite fish. 'Hello Nelson,' he boomed, 'come and have a yarn with Johnny Walker and me.' Johnny Walker is the wine merchant's cat. A young tabby, who earned his name by always curling up for a snooze in an empty Johnny Walker whisky case.

This Merchant Navy Cats Club came into being when Ma Flynn decided that they also serve who only keep the rats at bay. After all, the Merchant Navy humans had the missions to seamen, so why not something for nautical cats. Nelson had just downed a sardine and gulped some milk when there was a disturbance at the door. Three mean, vicious looking alley cats had appeared with predatory eyes on the sardines. Now, although he's not as young as he'd like to be; when it comes to the old eyeball to eyeball confrontation, with arched back, straight tail, a snarl and a spit, Nelson can still hold his own with the best of them. Prowler Pete, the resident bouncer, rose to his full height.

He is a huge black cat, bearing the scars of countless encounters in sea ports all over the world. 'Come on lads,' he said and together with Nelson, Kipper and Johnny Walker, went straight into action. A large, evil looking black and white tom hurled himself at Nelson who stood his ground and got in first with a well-aimed south-paw blow to his assailant's head. The evil stray retaliated with an uppercut to Nelson's nose and whiskers. It hurt, but the injured sea cat moved into a blocking position again, as the persistent intruder tried to round him and get to the sardines and milk.

All around, the air was thick with snarls and spit. Prowler quickly sent one of the marauding trio scooting off out of harm's way and Nelson after striking once again with his left paw, put another one to flight. One final alley-cat remained battling furiously with Kipper, who retreated momentarily dazed. This gave the alley-cat an opportunity to seize a sardine and quickly make off before Prowler could reach him.

The victorious sea cats then returned to their favourite spot around the stove. Johnny Walker said, 'Gosh Nelson, I wish I could go to sea and become tough and respected like you and Prowler.'

'What? Leave a nice safe little job with the wine merchant, for the uncertainty of a life at sea?' queried Nelson.

'I could tell you tales that would make your whiskers curl!' Johnny Walker looking wistful said, 'I'd still like to get away on a long sea voyage to prove myself, but please tell me about some of your experiences Nelson.'

'Come over here then Johnny and rest your timbers, whilst I tell you how I got my name and how I first slipped my cable out of Liverpool docks many years ago,' said the old sea cat.

Nelson's story

I was born in the back alleys of Liverpool docklands where the plaintive tooting of ship sirens was my nightly lullaby. As I grew up, it was to a hard life of raiding the dustbins and living on my wits, in much the same way as those alley cats we just put to flight. I was fast becoming a hardened criminal when a stroke of good fortune came my way and altered the whole course of my life.

One morning, I was up at sunrise and out and about on my normal food hunting activities, when a delicious smell of fresh fish made my nostrils twitch. It came from a lorry parked outside a large cold-storage depot. I measured the height of the lorry's platform with a quick glance and then leapt onto the rear, just as it moved off. This was a ride I hadn't intended to take and unfortunately the fish was packed in crates and completely paw-proof. The vehicle was now moving too fast for me to jump off, so I sat still, waiting to see what would happen. After a short journey, the lorry began to slow down at the entrance to Huskisson Dock, one of a long line of docks which formed the Port of Liverpool. This was my opportunity and I cleared the back of the lorry in one bound, landing safely on all four paws. The driver was asking the policeman at the gate the whereabouts of a liner, for which the fish was intended as ship stores. The lorry moved off again and I was left confronting a short, stout, jolly looking dock policeman. He called to me, 'Puss puss puss, come here, I won't harm you, nice pussy cat,' etc. The usual fawning drivel they seem to favour when addressing our kind. As always, I was on guard and ready to disappear quickly if threatened, but he appeared to be quite genuine, so I allowed him to approach and to stroke me. He said, 'You're a fine ginger tom, just like the moggy I knew on a Nelson line ship.'

'Nelson Moggy,' he continued, 'that's what we'll call you.' He picked me up, took me to his hut and set down a saucer of milk. I was overwhelmed. I'd never received this kind of treatment before, and I suddenly realised how thirsty I'd become. I lapped up the milk eagerly and even managed a contented purr. The policeman, Joe Strickland by name, adopted me and we became good friends. I was happy to use his cosy hut as my base and gradually, 'Nelson Moggy' became well known in the Huskisson dock area. I saw many seamen passing the hut, some going on shore leave, others returning to their ships to commence the next voyage. It was all very exciting; the bustle of dockworkers, the lorries arriving with cargoes for shipment, the smell of ship's paint and the special tang of the Mersey river, leading to the open sea. I was fascinated by the ships of all nations, which came to this great port; the distinctive shapes and colours of their funnels and the proud house flags flying from their fore-masts. The whole atmosphere was affecting me and beginning to forge the shape of my destiny.

One day a rather jaunty looking sea-faring cat, a sleek tabby, paused by the hut, on his way to the dock area. He introduced himself as 'Rodney'. Sea cats of course, do not have landlubber names such as 'Tiddles' and 'Fluff'. He told me some fur-raising tales about his long voyages to the more exotic places in the world. His description of shipboard life, with cosy berths in the galley, plenty of food and quick furtive trips ashore in foreign ports, was music to my ears. When he suggested I go with him to have a look at his ship, I readily agreed. We padded along, close to the water's edge until we came to two fine looking cargo passenger liners. The first one was called S.S Magellan and standing at the top of the ship's gangway was a black and white cat, with the most unusual markings. A large black circle around the nose area and shiny white whiskers either side of his nostrils. I commented on this to Rodney and said, 'You know the facial features remind me of some kind of musical instrument.'

'Yes,' agreed Rodncy, 'thc captain thought the same and decided to call his ship's cat Banjo-face, and that's what he's known as throughout the fleet.'

'Poor cat,' I said. 'I don't think I'd like to sail the seven seas burdened with a name like that.'

The other liner S.S Cape Horn, lying just ahead, was Rodney's ship. He proudly ushered me aboard. It was the first time I'd ever been on a ship and my nose was assailed by a multitude of smells. I detected that the interior had been recently repainted and the smell of oil, coffee, pastries, tobacco, wines and spirits etc, mingled excitedly. I followed Rodney down companionways into the bowels of the ship and to the galley, which was his preferred territory. Here, the appetising smell of food was much stronger and I was invited to share Rodney's liberally heaped plate of bacon scraps with mashed potato and his bowl of milk. The galley crew greeted us good-naturedly and I realised that the ship's cat of S.S Cape Horn was well established.

This visit was enough to convince me that sea-faring was in my blood and after the Cape Horn had sailed, I prowled around the docks day after day looking for a likely ship. I was beginning to despair when an opportunity finally came my way. A tramp-ship called the 'Ocean Vagabond' was without a ship's cat. Her long-serving faithful moggy of many voyages had disappeared shortly after the ship docked and had not been seen since. The vessel was rusty, in need of a coat of paint and had obviously seen better days, but she was my first ship and I gratefully scuttled aboard. The crew welcomed me and I was given a chipped but serviceable food bowl, and a blanket placed in a cosy corner of the galley. I brightened up the prevailing gloom a little, since it was a bad omen for their cat to desert the ship. They remembered tales of another famous ship's cat, Dowie of the 'Lusitania', who climbed down a hawser and disappeared into the shadows of New York docks in the USA on 1st May 1915. The 'Lusitania' duly sailed but seven days later was sunk by a German submarine off the south coast of Ireland. It was one of the tragic maritime disasters of World War I.

My voyage on 'Ocean Vagabond' was little better. The ship sank in a hurricane after leaving Jamaica in the West Indies, with a full cargo of rum in kegs. I was thrown into the sea and only survived by clinging to a floating life-raft with other crew members. We were eventually picked up by a passing liner, whose sharp-eyed officer of the watch had reported our distress to his ship's captain. Since then, I have been all over the world on passenger liners, freighters, tramp-ships and oil-tankers. We ships' cats are of great importance in the British Mercantile Marine and very few vessels put to sea these days without a nautical cat aboard.

A faraway look appeared in Nelson's yellow-green eyes at the end of his story.

He envied the young sea cats bidding farewell at Ma Flynn's and setting off on yet another voyage. His mood on such occasions might best be described in a few lines from Kipling's 'The Long Trail'

'And I'd sell my tired soul
for the bucking beam sea roll
of a black Bilbao tramp'.

My Messy Room

Carole Morris

It was one of those days.

'I am bored,' said Rhys, 'what can I do?'

Rhys stood by his cupboard as he looked for something to do. 'Oh dear,' he sighed. Then he remembered his marbles. Where had he put them? He could not quite remember.

Rhys pulled a chair towards his cupboard and stretched up high and began to take everything out of his cupboard and laid them out onto his bedroom floor. He bumped and banged and soon Rhys' room was full of clutter, but he had still not found his marbles.

Where have I put those marbles, he asked himself.

He climbed down from the chair and began to empty his toy box as he looked around the room he realised what a mess he had made. Rhys scratched his curly head, then he knelt by his bed and lifted up the bed clothes and peered under.

'Yes!' he said, 'they were here all the time.'

There were other things there as well, like empty crisp packets, sweet papers and one of Rhys' smelly socks.

It was not long before Rhys' mum came up to see what all the noise was about and what a fright she had when she popped her head around the door.

'Rhys tidy your room up please, it is in a terrible mess,' his mum said.

He put his marbles into a clear container and left them on his window sill then he began to clear the mess up off the floor.

Rhys put the things he wanted away into the cupboard then he put the things he did not want onto the landing and soon his room was tidy again and when his mum came up to see, the mess was all gone and she was very pleased with Rhys.

'Well done,' she said, 'I think you deserve a little pocket money for making a very good effort in tidying your room.'

He took his marbles down from the window sill and looked at the coins in his hand. 'Wow!' said Rhys, 'pocket money.' He was very pleased with himself. 'Thanks,' he said, 'I was not bored after all, I did find something to do!'

KATIE AND THE LITTLE OWL
Christine Hardemon

As the moonlight crept through Katie's bedroom window, she moved restlessly in her bed. Soon however, she woke up and as she raised her golden head she spotted almost at once a little owl sitting at the end of her cosy bed. He was a magic owl with big round sparkling eyes.

Katie was a little frightened at first and peeped over the duvet. Then to her surprise he spoke in a gentle sort of way, 'Hello Katie, happy birthday.'

She rubbed her eyes in amazement and joy to make sure she wasn't dreaming. Today was her fifth birthday and the little owl had brought her a present. It was a tiny doll, no bigger than your thumb.

'Close your eyes,' he continued in his gentle way, 'I'll take you on a magic trip for your birthday.'

He put his wings around her as she closed her eyes and when she opened them she had shrunk to the size of the little owl. Gently she climbed onto his downy back and off into the sky he flew.

She clasped the little owl tightly as they sped across the sky. It was very dark now as they flew on up high. Katie wondered what her mum would say when she discovered she had gone, but these thoughts soon escaped her mind because she was so excited to be flying through the sky with Little Owl.

At long last they reached an enormous wood where wild animals lived and played. Katie knew that they would stay here for a while.

Suddenly a long-eared bat flew past her head and she let out a little squeal. Little Owl flew to a nearby tree and paused to rest with Katie sitting safely on his knee.

Katie glanced around in amazement, for the wood was golden and not just shades of brown and green. First she spotted a little mouse out with its family for a stroll. She hugged her little doll tightly as she slipped from Little Owl's back onto the soft earth. A badger appeared with its nose firmly fixed to the ground looking for earthworms for his supper.

She held her breath in excitement - she didn't want to make a sound. A red squirrel collecting nuts scampered across the clearing, then she spotted a roe deer nervously peering from behind a bush. Rabbits hopped across the grass, Katie watched them playing chase and laughed out loud. There were several rabbits, it looked like a mother with four youngsters.

Suddenly they all vanished down a rabbit hole, for the smell of fox came drifting past on the night air. Katie held her breath as a young fox silently crept into her view. His nose twitched as he smelt the rabbits that had been there only a few seconds before. Then as silently as he had arrived he disappeared into the undergrowth.

Her friendly owl whispered in her ear, 'It's time we went on our way Katie dear.'

She was sad to leave this magical place but knew that the little owl was right. So she clasped the little owl tightly as he took flight.

Soon they were whizzing further into the wood. At first Katie thought she was going back home, but her adventure had only just begun and there would still be more surprises. As she clung to Little Owl's wings she knew that there would be more treats in store for her on her special birthday.

They swiftly flew through the wood and very soon Katie spotted a golden cottage in the distance. Now the sun was beginning to rise and the cottage shone brightly in the sunlight. Little Owl flew towards the cottage and landed safely on the ground. The golden cottage was surrounded by flowers of every colour. Red roses nodded their heads around the door, pink carnations - their aroma very strong stood tall along with hollyhocks and lupins.

Little Owl spoke to Katie in his gentle way, 'Open the golden latch on the door.'

Katie walked to the door and pushed very hard. The door opened and she stared inside. Katie stood amazed at the sight that met her eyes for it was like looking into fairyland, and of course it was fairyland.

Little Owl flew through the door and spoke to Katie, 'We shall go and meet some of the fairies who live here.'

Katie walked through the door and followed him down the winding path. In the distance she could see little toadstools all brightly coloured, yellow and red, pink and purple with tiny little windows and doors. Pretty curtains hung at the windows and each toadstool had its own garden neatly filled with flowers. Katie was very excited as sitting on the doorstop of one of the toadstools was a tiny fairy with pink and purple wings. Her name was Crocus, she looked again and outside the yellow and red toadstool was a fairy with yellow and red wings.

Little Owl explained that the fairies all had their own toadstool homes painted to match their wings. Little Owl hopped over to Crocus fairy with the pink and purple wings and she looked up at him and smiled.

'Hello Little Owl who is this young visitor you've brought to fairyland?'

'This is Katie and today is her special day, because it's her fifth birthday,' replied Little Owl.

'Oh how exciting,' Crocus squealed in her tiny voice, 'I must go and tell all my friends.' And with that she flew off gracefully into the air.

Katie watched her go - amazed at the fairy flying so high into the brightly lit sky. Now Little Owl went and gently tapped on another toadstool door, a little red and yellow fairy appeared, she said her name was Bluebell and was pleased to meet Katie.

Katie walked down the rows of neatly arranged gardens until she came to the last one which was not as neat as all the rest. She turned to look at Little Owl and he knew that she was puzzled by the end toadstool's appearance.

Suddenly his voice changed to sadness as he spoke of the fairy that lived there. Her name was Petal and she had flown off one day and never returned. All her fairy friends had flown high and low to find her and couldn't trace her anywhere. It had been two weeks now since she had disappeared and they were hoping that very soon she would fly home. What could have happened to her - no one knew.

Katie was puzzled by this too and thought she would like to help to find Petal.

Little Owl looked at Katie remembering that this was her special day and he spoke in his gentle way, 'Come on Katie hop on my back as we have much to do today.'

By now Katie was enjoying her birthday so much - however at the back of her mind she kept remembering the fairy Petal - where was she?

Little Owl flew on for a while then in the distance Katie spotted lots of tiny figures on the ground. As Little Owl landed fairies and pixies cheered and musicians started to play Happy Birthday. The musicians were field mice all dressed in blue uniforms playing tiny trumpets, drums, violins - musical instruments of every kind. Tiny horses with wings were flying around ready to take the pixies on rides.

It was a wonderful sight and Katie was so pleased that this had all been arranged for her special birthday. Little Owl took Katie to one of the fairies who was sitting at a sewing machine making lots of tiny clothes for the fairies and pixies to wear. The fairy handed Katie a silver dress for her tiny doll (which was no bigger than your thumb) to wear.

Suddenly Little Owl said excitedly, 'Petal is it really you? Why we've been so worried about you and all the time you were here making a special silver dress for Katie's doll and one for Katie too.'

Petal smiled and said she was sorry she had caused everyone to be worried about her and she would be going home soon - to tidy up her garden.

It was a wonderful party for Katie. There were pieces of cheese for the mice musicians to eat and lots of fairy cakes which the fairies had made themselves. Honey had been diluted and was drunk from tiny buttercup heads and of course there was a birthday cake for Katie with five candles on the top for her to blow out.

Soon it was time for Katie to climb aboard the little owl's back and return home. She was sad to be leaving all her new friends but had had a wonderful birthday, one which she would never forget.

Up on Little Owl's back she sat, with Petal, Bluebell, Crocus and all the other fairies and pixies waving bye-bye as up into the sky he flew.

First Little Owl would have to pass through the door of the golden cottage and then on through the magic wood - where wild animals lived and played.

At long last they arrived back in the magic wood, it seemed to Katie that time had stood still and that she hadn't been very far, but this was the magic wood and now there was the journey ahead to her home. Katie clung tightly to the little owl as he soared in the sky, soon they would reach her home and her adventure would be over.

Katie recognised her garden far below and in no time at all Little Owl landed softly on her window sill. He hopped down into her bedroom and she climbed from his back. A tear appeared in his eye as Little Owl wrapped his wings around Katie to wish her goodbye. She closed her eyes and whispered in his ear, 'Bye Little Owl, I've had the most wonderful birthday ever, I hope that you'll come and visit me again.' When she opened her eyes she was surprised to see Little Owl flying high in the sky and to her amazement she had returned to her normal size.

Then she heard her mum and dad calling her name, ‘Katie, Katie dear, happy birthday,’ and they both rushed into her room.

‘Oh!’ said her mum. ‘This is a very pretty doll and what a beautiful dress, where did this come from?’

Katie smiled to herself - it was her and Little Owl’s secret - and yours.

Three French Marigolds

Sylvia Scoville

In my garden grew some orange flowers called *French Marigolds.* They opened their petals as the sun rose in the morning. Their leaves quivered as they shook the dewdrops off. When the sun moved round the garden, the French Marigolds turned their heads and stretched their necks to be above the blue aubretia and kept their faces pointed to the sun.

Cherie, the first marigold in the row said, 'My petals are firmer than yours.'

Francine, the second marigold said, 'Maybe. But my petals are nearly gold and shine better than yours.'

Petula, who was standing tall and upright said, 'You two make me sick! My perfume is the sweetest smell of all and that is what the humans like the best. I've also got more flowers on my stems. In the morning, I'll be the one to be picked for the show and get *first prize* . . . you see!'

The next morning dawned . . .

There was no sight of the three proud marigolds. *Slugs* had eaten them.

Pierre, a beautiful French Marigold won *first prize*. He was growing in a special pot standing on the window sill.

* * *

Easop fable: 'Pride comes before a fall'.

Do you know anyone who is boastful?

Mr Jolly's New Hat

Kathleen Townsley

Have you ever wondered what happens to the happy, smiling snowmen when they disappear each spring? Well, let me tell you . . .

One night when the sky is bright and starry, whilst all good girls and boys are fast asleep in their beds, a call comes to the snowmen and they raise their heads in answer. It is a call that you or I will never hear, yet, if you happened to peep out of your bedroom window at precisely the right time you would be amazed, for walking down each street, lane or avenue, arm in arm, in groups of three or four, are lines upon lines of snowmen. They are chatting away merrily, greeting every new snowman they meet, on their way to an enchanted door, a door that we will never see, but it beckons the snowmen home. Behind the door are hundreds of sleighs waiting to take the snowmen back to their place of birth, which if you have not already guessed is Santa Land, for that is where the snowmen come from each year to surprise all the children in the land. This is all so that when you rise one cold and snowy morning, open your curtains and look down upon the fallen snow, you will see a smiling, jolly snowman looking right back up at you.

You will see a snowman with a wobbly, round body, a big happy face with a carrot nose and button eyes with a big smile made of shiny black coal. He will also have a wobbly double chin, a multicoloured scarf around his neck with a matching bob hat and stick-like arms with gloves on. This is the most amazing sight to wake up to.

Arm in arm the snowmen continue walking down each street and lane till they see the shining red door. They step through the door, climb aboard the sleighs and with a blink of an eye they are once again in Santa's Land amongst the families they all love. Waiting to welcome them home are all the fairies and elves who help Santa all year in his workshops. These are the snowmen's best friends, even though they have been busy helping Santa over the Christmas time, they look forward to the return of their friends from the kingdom of the children. They are all excited when spring approaches for they know their dear friends, the snowmen, will be coming home. As you know, snowmen disappear in spring, but children all know that they will return again when snow once again begins to fall. The snowmen greet their friends with great joy, full of the stories to tell of their time in the kingdom of children; the games they played and the games the children played, each one has a tale to tell, but I will tell you of one snowman that lost his hat.

It was snowing heavy when the children came out to play, and after they had said good morning to Mr Jolly, for that is what the children had called him, they commenced a snowball fight in the garden. Mr Jolly watched the snowballs flying past his nose hoping that they did not knock his carrot nose off and if by chance they did, wondered if it would be lost amongst the falling snow. Listening to the children's squeals of laughter, he forgot all about the snow fight and enjoyed the morning's fun, storing away the information to tell all his friends when he returned home.

As the children went inside to play, for the snow had begun to fall heavier, he smiled to himself and, closing his eyes, settled down to an afternoon nap. Watching the children playing was exhausting for Mr Jolly.

When he awoke it was to feel a cold wind blowing around his head. *My, my,* he thought, *it is a cold wind coming from Santa Land this evening*. With horror he realised his hat had gone. What to do, he wondered, for he knew his friends, the elves, had knitted all the hats and scarves for the snowmen and he was so proud of his multicoloured bob hat. His gloves were still on his hands and the scarf was still fastened around his neck, but his lovely matching bob hat was gone.

When the children came out to play the following day they noticed Mr Jolly's smile was tilting down at each corner and he had icicles on his head. The children ran back indoors and brought out a grown-up. Mr Jolly was not too sure of grown-ups for he rarely met grown-ups. The children were talking away to the grown-up who just kept nodding its head. Soon they all went back into the house. After a few minutes the grown-up came back out and put a string around Mr Jolly's head, then taking out of a pocket a shiny object, the grown-up cut the string. The grown-up and the children all went back inside. Mr Jolly sat and looked at the windows of the house. The wind was blowing harder and deep inside Mr Jolly shivered, for without his lovely hat the wind made his whole head cold and we all know if your head is cold it makes you shiver.

He awoke again after his afternoon nap to see the snow had stopped falling and the wind had stopped blowing. Although he was still cold, his head felt warm again. The children were running towards Mr Jolly, followed by the grown-up.

When they circled Mr Jolly, the children said, 'Mr Jolly, Mummy has a present for you, for being our best friend.'

Then the grown-up (he now knew as Mummy) showed him a multi-stripped bob hat; yellow, red, green, purple, blue and white. Hanging down from each side were multicoloured lengths of wool. Placing the hat on his head, Mummy gathered all the threads together and tied them under his chin with a big bow.

'There Mr Jolly, that will keep it safe on your head and stop the wind and snowballs from knocking it off,' Mummy the grown-up said. Turning, she went back towards the house.

'Mr Jolly, you look lovely,' the children said. 'Wait till all our friends see you, for you are the best in the avenue and we love you.' The children gave Mr Jolly a hug, then ran back inside, for evening was drawing near.

Mr Jolly waited till he saw the children's light go on in their bedroom then, tilting his head upwards he smiled widely for the children always waved down to Mr Jolly, shouting 'night, night'. They had done this since Mr Jolly had arrived in their garden.

Later, when all was silent, he called over to his friend in the next garden who said he thought Mr Jolly's hat was fantastic. It really looked nice on Mr Jolly. What a story he could tell Santa on his return to Santa Land.

When every snowman returned home in spring, Santa loved to hear all their stories, and every evening, the fairies and elves gathered round. One snowman was selected to tell a tale from their days in the kingdom of children. This they did every evening on their return and, because there were thousands of snowmen, they had enough stories to keep everyone happy till the time came for them to return to the kingdom of the children.

One day, Mr Jolly noticed a change in the wind. A warmer breeze blew around his feet. Oh yes, snowmen have feet, but you cannot see them for they only appear when it is time to go home. He knew spring was coming and soon he would hear the calling from Santa to come home. Although he was sad to leave the children, he was also excited at going home for he missed his friends and was looking forward to seeing them all again, and most of all to see Santa.

When he arrived back in Santa Land, he was the first to be chosen to tell his story, for everyone had noticed his new hat.

When he had finished his tale, Santa said, 'Next winter you may return to the same garden.'

This surprised Mr Jolly for usually the snowmen changed places, allowing all the girls and boys to meet every snowman from Santa Land.

Time passed quickly and winter approached. The sleighs were summoned and the snowmen climbed aboard for their winter in the kingdom of children. Mr Jolly climbed into the sleigh. Santa gave him a little parcel and told him to leave it on the doorstep before he stood in his place in the garden.

The dawn broke and Mr Jolly looked up to the window, waiting for the children to rise from their beds. Soon the curtains opened and he heard the squeal of joy. As he waited patiently for the children to come and play, he wondered what Santa had given him. Then he heard a shout of joy and the door burst open.

The children ran into the garden and hugged him, saying, 'Thank you, Mr Jolly, for our lovely hat and scarf that you brought from Santa. Look, they are just the same as yours.'

Mr Jolly looked at the children, he could see they were indeed the same as his own multicoloured hat and scarf, just like the hat he had lost the year before.

'When you go home,' the children said, 'tell Santa thank you.' They ran back inside to get their coats.

Mr Jolly smiled and thought, *I will, I will indeed.*

You may wonder how I know of the snowmen. I am a friend of the fairies and the elves. It is my job to stand at the red door each year of calling and make sure every snowman has heard the call for Santa has many helpers, including a grown-up like me.

MR FOX GOES TO CHURCH

Patricia H Moore

Once upon a time in a tiny village, in the middle of a large town lived a grand fox. Fox was rather well-spoken and wore at all times a shiny red fur coat. Fox lived in the graveyard of the large and very old parish church, and his home could be found in one of the large tombs in the part referred to as the main triangle. Fox had moved to this new home four years ago after he had graduated from The Fox Academy, with his degree in animal leadership.

Mr Fox as he was called by all the other animals and birds in his neck of the woods, kept a very low profile at all times, but never the less he was always on hand for advice and a chat whenever it was needed from his fellow creatures. Although the other animals looked up to Mr Fox, he was known for his temper. Mr Fox could often be heard moaning and groaning about every little thing, and was often to be seen gossiping to one of the squirrels, usually about another member of the flock.

Mr Fox did not mix with the other animals, he kept himself to himself and in fact at times had nothing better to do than gossip. One night, just as the sun had fallen and the village had become still, news of a great celebration flowed through the graveyard, even the trees rustled their leaves with excitement. Each animal small and large began to prepare for this joyous party. The red-chested robin had finally announced the news of his wedding to a little bird, who was to join him from the vicar's garden.

They were to be married that night inside the belfry of the church at eleven o'clock and would make their home in the small triangle next to Fox. Mr Fox, who had just settled down for the night with some old scraps he had found that day, became annoyed by the noise outside and promptly went outside to investigate. Emerging from his home, he noticed that many birds were flying back and forth to the small triangle with twigs and leaves and mountains of food.

Fox found this most strange and walked slowly to the gate.

'I say,' said Fox in a rather loud voice, 'may I enquire, to the nature of all this fuss and noise?' Alas Fox could not be heard, for concentration was on the festivities.

Mr Fox did not like to be ignored and marched towards his home in disgust. Just then Squirrel came flying into Fox, dropping a large pile of acorns at his feet.

'I say Squirrel, less haste, you might have caused an accident,' Fox said crossly as he brushed himself off.

'Oh I am sorry Mr Fox, so much to do and so little time. Only ten more minutes to the wedding and nothing is at all ready,' said Squirrel in a panicked voice.

Fox looked rather puzzled, but continued his conversation to Squirrel. 'What wedding? I have heard nothing of these goings on, no one has consulted me on such matters!'

'I'm sorry Fox, didn't you know, Robin is to be married tonight to a well bred young bird who he has been flying with for months, did you not receive an invitation?' Squirrel asked carefully.

'I dare say one did, however as I have been out all day and have not yet been home, it may be that one was dropped off earlier,' Fox announced, knowing that this was not true as he had been in all night. Squirrel then hurried on, forgetting even to bid Fox a good night.

Poor Fox wandered home to the sound of celebration and singing from the small triangle. Mr Fox could not understand why Robin had not sent him an invitation to his wedding, after all he was the head of the graveyard and he had given him much advice over the past years. Still Fox believed this to be an oversight and planned to speak to Robin first thing in the morning . . .

The following morning Fox awoke to the sound of the church bells ringing. It was Sunday, Fox's favourite day. He would hide behind a stone and watch people arrive for the service, dressed in their good clothes and fancy hats. Once the service had begun, Fox would move as close to the doors as possible to hear the sound of the singing coming from inside. As Fox approached the doors he noticed that both sets of swing doors were open, which gave him a good view of inside.

Fox had forgotten that he was going to see Robin, but instead summoned all his courage and very quietly and slowly crept inside the church. So as not to be seen. Fox sat just by the inside door, ready to make a quick move if he was spotted.

In the pulpit he could see the vicar talking to the people that had arrived earlier and so Fox began to listen. As Fox heard the word, he dropped his head, for now Fox realised why Robin had not invited him to the wedding.

Fox remembered that he had, two days before gossiped about Robin's affairs to Barney the bumblebee and the things he had spoken were very unkind. Fox, with his head still lowered in shame, turned and walked slowly back to his home. Fox spent hours worrying and wondering how he could make things right, and then he remembered what the vicar had said about asking for forgiveness.

All at once Fox fell to his knees, and putting both paws together prayed that the Lord would forgive him for what he had said. Fox also realised that this, although right, would not be enough to solve the problem between Robin and himself.

Fox set out once again to the home of Robin redbreast. Fox had never had to say sorry before and was finding it hard to know what to say. As he approached he noticed Robin tending his nest.

'Robin, old chap, I was hoping that I might have a word, regarding your marriage,' Fox said rather boldly.

'If you have come here to give me advice Mr Fox, it is too late and I am not sure that I am at all interested,' said Robin, not even looking up from his work.

Fox looked to the ground and rather nervously continued, 'Well er . . . er . . . it actually is like this, I believe that I may have hurt you in some way, well no, actually I know I did, and I would like to ask your forgiveness for the unkind things I said to Bumblebee.' There was a long silence, until Fox added, 'There is no excuse for my behaviour and I would not blame you if you never spoke to me again, but I realise what I have done is wrong and how it must have hurt you and I am extremely sorry.'

Robin lifted his head and flew down to the feet of Mr Fox. 'I accept your apology, for it is a brave thing that you have done, not many creatures can admit they are wrong or even say sorry. If you are prepared to change your ways, then, what has happened in the past I will forget,' Robin said gently.

With that both Robin and Fox walked around the graveyard, sharing and chatting, not just amongst themselves but also to fellow neighbours and friends. Fox began a new life, and made many new friends, he was never bored and never found the need to gossip ever again . . .

Years later, Fox could be found on the eve of Robin's wedding anniversary telling this tale, to all the young siblings gathered around him. And it was so at the end of the tale, a small wing or a small paw would shoot high in the air and present the same question.

'Mr Fox, Mr Fox, do please tell us, what is it that we should take away from this story?'

'Ah,' said Fox as he removes his spectacles and lifts his paw in the air. 'The moral of this story, for every boy and girl, when speaking to another, kind words you must employ for, if not a thing that you can say, is nice and true and kind, close your lips and do not speak, for friendship you will find. And if you find, you've let your tongue, speak horrible that day, then ask the Lord above you to forgive you when you pray. And never be too frightened to say that you are sorry. Believe me when I tell you it saves a lot of worry.'

REWOPOTMOT

Julie Lewis

'Who are you?' yelled Tom as he scrambled to the top of his bed. He had been reading his comic a few minutes before when he had a feeling that someone was watching him. The end of his bed had felt heavy. That was when he had looked up and saw the little man sitting on the other end.

'Please don't shout.' The tiny person covered his ears with his hands.

'Sorry,' whispered Tom.

He looked at the little man again. He was about the same size as himself but looked older, at least as old as his grandad. His face was thin, his nose large. His eyes were bright green and twinkled. He wore trainers, jeans, a baseball cap on back to front and a sweatshirt with writing on it. The writing read, *'Rewop ot mot'*.

'Must be a foreign language,' Tom thought out loud.

'Must it now,' the little man was smiling.

'I asked you who you are?' Tom wondered what his mum would say if she found him in his bedroom.

'I'm an alf,' said the little man.

'A what?' asked Tom puzzled.

'We used to be called elves, you know an elf, a boy fairy.'

'I don't believe in fairies. They are stories for little kids.'

'Not true,' grinned the little man. 'I'm an elf. Our leader said we were too old fashioned and decided to make us look modern. That's why we wear these clothes. He changed our names to alfs. You can call me Alf if you like Tom.'

'How do you know who I am? What are you doing in my bedroom? How did you get here?' The questions tumbled out one after another.

'That's a lot of questions. First, I know your name because my leader sent me. You are my assignment.'

'What's an assignment?' Tom loved new words.

'Well, an assignment is a task. You are my task. As to how I got here, I came on a lightbeam. We don't use wings anymore, too slow. Your mum and dad don't believe in fairies you know.'

'I don't believe in them either. I told you that already,' Tom reminded him.

‘You believe in aliens so why not alfs?’ Alf looked very hurt.

‘What do the words on your T-shirt mean?’ Tom changed the subject quickly. Alf was right. He did believe in aliens. ‘Is it French?’

Alf started to laugh. He laughed so much he fell off the bed.

‘Don’t make so much noise. My mum will hear you.’

‘She can’t hear me.’ Alf climbed back onto Tom’s bed still grinning. ‘The writing is in code. Break the code and you will understand why I am here.’

Tom looked at the words *’Rewop ot mot’*. They meant nothing.

‘I’m no good at puzzles. Can you give me a clue?’

‘OK, this riddle might help.’ Alf moved closer and chanted. ‘Dreams and wishes can come true if you know just what to do. Back to front not left to right, read the words and see the light.’

Tom looked at the words and said the rhyme over and over. ‘Words back to front,’ he muttered to himself. ‘Wow! That’s it. *Rewop* back to front reads *power.’*

Alf nodded grinning.

‘How clever. If I turn the rest around it reads, *ot,* that’s *to. Mot,* that’s *Tom. Power to Tom.’*

Alf clapped loudly, pleased Tom had worked it out.

‘But what does it mean?’

Alf sighed. ‘Before I tell you that. Tell me what you did after school today?’

Tom frowned. ‘Well, I came home from school, changed my clothes then read a comic and watched telly until teatime. That’s what I always do.’

‘Why don’t you go out and play with your friends?’ Alf stared at him.

Tom bent his head. ‘I don’t have many friends. No one wants to play with me.’

‘Why?’ asked Alf.

‘The boys call me bookworm because I like to read. They all play football after school. They are football crazy, it’s all they ever talk about.’

Alf asked Tom if he liked football?

‘Yes I do. I love watching football on the telly with my dad. Sometimes we go to see a real match. My favourite team is Danchester.’ Tom became excited as he talked.

Alf asked him why if he liked football so much, didn't he play with his friends?

'Mum says I have two left feet. I spend more time on the ground than I do kicking the ball. I'm hopeless. The boys laugh and tell me to go away.' Tom spoke very quietly.

'Now you know why I am here,' said Alf. 'You made a wish and here I am.'

Tom stared at him. He remembered making a wish that afternoon. He had wished he could be in the park playing football.

'I can't see how you can help me?' He didn't think wishes came true any more than he believed in fairies.

'I want to be your friend Tom so believe what I tell you. *'Rewop ot mot'* are magical words. Believe in them and you can do anything. That means if you want to play football with your friends you only have to say the words and it will happen.'

Tom's mouth fell open. He stared at Alf. He did so want to believe it would all happen.

'Do you really think the boys will let me play with them?'

'Ask them. It's all part of the magic. You have to believe in yourself. Only you can make it happen.'

Alf sounded far away. Tom closed his eyes and hugged his knees. It would be wonderful if it came true.

Tom opened his eyes. The sun was shining and it was Saturday and he was going to spend his birthday money on having a special T-shirt printed.

'Whatever made me think of that?' muttered Tom to himself. Then he remembered Alf. He didn't remember him saying goodbye, or leaving. He wouldn't tell his mum and dad about Alf, they would only say he'd been dreaming.

'Mum, are you going shopping today?' Tom asked him mum when he saw her.

His mum looked up from the toast she was buttering. 'Yes I'm going this morning.'

'I want to go to the high street please. I want to buy a T-shirt with my birthday money.'

'You have so many, why another one?' his mum sounded surprised.

'I want a special one,' Tom said gulping down his breakfast.

Tom and his mum went to a shop in town called 'Print Me'. He could hardly stand still he was so excited.

'Can you print these words in black on a white T-shirt please?' Tom grinned.

'Sure can. That will be five pounds. What does it mean?' the shopkeeper frowned as he looked at the letters Tom had joined together to make one word.

'Rewopotmot goodness Tom what does that mean?' Tom's mum had only just seen the letters.

'I can't tell you. It's a secret code.' He wasn't going to tell anyone what the letters meant.

The shopkeeper printed the shirt and showed Tom.

'Brilliant.' He thanked the man, paid his money and left the shop.

When Tom got home he rushed up to his bedroom and hid the T-shirt. He did so want to tell his mum and dad about Alf but wasn't sure they would understand.

After school on Monday Tom went straight to his bedroom, changed into his jeans, put on his trainers and his new *'Rewopotmot'* T-shirt.

'I want to play,' he whispered.

The boys stopped their game. They were surprised to see him. Joe and Tim started whispering to each other. Tom saw them and his heart sank. Those two were always laughing at him. Once again he rubbed the letters on his shirt. Alf had said he was to believe in himself.

'Hi! Can I play?' Tom waited hardly daring to breathe. He expected the boys to tell him to clear off. They didn't.

'OK,' said Peter, the leader. 'You will have to go out on the wing. Funny writing on your shirt Tom?'

'Mm,' muttered Tom running off to the side of the field.

Tom looked at the two jumpers placed far enough apart on the ground to make a goal. If only he could score. For a while, the ball didn't go anywhere near him, still at least he was playing and that was quite something. Then the ball was coming straight at him. He hoped he wouldn't fall over and spoil things.

'Rewopotnot,' Tom whispered, rubbing both hands over the letters. Raising his foot he stopped the ball and started to dribble it towards the goal. All the while he was running he kept repeating, *'Rewopotmot, Rewopotmot.'* He raced past Tim, then Joe. In front of him was the goal.

Tom kicked as hard as he could. The ball went past the goalkeeper and between the two jumpers.

'Goal! Goal! Wow wee!' Peter was slapping Tom on the back. 'That was brilliant. I didn't know you could run like that. Why haven't you come to play before? We need you.'

'Does that mean you will let me play tomorrow?' Tom had been afraid to ask in case Peter said no.

'Of course. Come on let's play.' Peter kicked the ball to start the game again.

The rest of the boys congratulated Tom, even Tim and Joe said how well he had played.

That evening Tom told his mum what had happened at the park. She was pleased for him. She knew he hadn't many friends.

'I knew you had it in you, well done,' said his dad when he heard about the goal.

In bed that night Tom put his hands behind his head and closed his eyes. He was thinking about everything that had happened at the park. He opened his eyes when he heard a tiny cough.

'Alf! It's you? I thought I would never see you again. Today I played football with the boys and I scored a goal. They want me to play again tomorrow. It's all thanks to you.' Tom could hardly breathe in his excitement to tell Alf what had happened.

'It was down to you, not me. I just showed you what you could do if you wanted to.' Alf was sitting crossed legged on Tom's bed. 'If you ever need help again, think of me and I will come.'

'Thanks. Would you like to see my T-shirt? I joined all the letters together so no one could guess what it said.' He picked up his shirt to show Alf. Alf had gone.

Tom was sad. He still didn't believe Alf was an elf or rather an alf. But whoever he was Tom liked him and his magic had worked. That was all that mattered and his secret code word *'Rewopotmot'*.

CAPTAIN BOBBITT AND THE CURSE OF THE CRYSTAL EYE

Glenwyn Evans

Lord Ruthless Dungbeetle, wanted the throne of Bugland, and so, along with his accomplice, Lizard-Wizard, Evm, formed a sinister plot, to blast Her Majesty, Queen Bee, into smithereens . . . However, the plot blew up in Dungbeetle's face, and, needing a name to blame, he dramatically, pinned it on the Queen's favourite flee-actor, Errol Flea.

But Errol, realising that something was drastically wrong, escaped . . .

Now, a very wanted flea, he sought refuge in the beautiful land of fairies and elves, and changed his name to William Kidd Bobbitt; it was here that Good Queen Jean, on hearing the evil tidings of Queen Bee's plight, and the capture of Lady Byrd Bird, asked William if he'd rescue them . . . And from that adventure, our gallant hero, Captain Bobbitt, became the Guardian of the Golden Secret . . . In a golden locket, that now hung his neck . . . The prize? The golden land of El Bug'rado, itself . . .

It was this that Evm Lizard-Wizard, suddenly realised he'd let slip, through his slippery mitts . . . But what could they do now? Both were locked in Dungbeetle's own dungeons, awaiting their executions.

Death, stared them in the face . . .

The first guard, pulled his face, grimly, thus, producing a long tape measure:

'E's gotta t-r-e-m-e-n-d-o-u-s nut!'

'Aye,' agreed the other, sharpening the blade of his axe. Dungbeetle glowered, cursing Evm. What happened to all his powers being restored? Fishzooks!

'Hey!' snorted the first guard, with a prod. 'Yeah ain't a cockroach . . . are yer?'

'That's a thought,' interrupted the second, pondering the situation, thoroughly. 'Only, we already got one of them screaming cockroaches . . . it haunts the Tottering Tower, screaming.'

'How can a headless cockroach, scream?' snorted Dungbeetle, contemptuously.

'So's, yer are a cockroach, then?'

'No! I'm a dungbeetle,' snapped his lordship. 'And have I not seen you idiots somewhere before?'

'Don't be gormless,' snapped the second guard, fiercely, producing a very large black scarf.

'There'll be no need for blindfolds,' insisted his lordship, gruffly, holding up the palm of his mitt, in a bold act of defiance.

'Tut-tut-tut,' spluttered the first guard. 'S'not for you, tis for us.'

'Yeah, if it's one thing that we woodlice can't stand, it's the sight of blood . . . well, in your case, beetle juice,' chortled the second, with a swish of the axe.

Dungbeetle's antennae, jerked, frantically.

'Be careful wit' tha' f'ing,' spat the first. 'Yer nearly took this poor bloke's 'ead off!' Now, bend yer knees yer Lordship, and drop thee noggin on the 'x' mark, and, wit' a bi' o' luck, me bro', might just take yer 'ead off in one blow . . .'

'One blow?' scolded Dungbeetle, angrily. 'Luck?'

'Well, we are wearing our best blindfolds, yer lordship,' declared the second, sympathetically. Dungbeetle, protested with a long, nauseating fart.

'Donna worry, Lordship,' said the first, producing two pegs for their noses. 'We woodlice come prepared . . . na, just 'old ye 'ead still, and me bro' 'ere, will swipe axe as gracefully as a pendulum striking der walls of a clock . . . O', I might add, that, If 'e, don't get yer by the sixth blow, 'e'll get yer on the seventh . . . Seven's our lucky number you see . . .'

'I knew it!' As his lordship's head went up and the axe chinked the stone chopped block, sparking, wildly.

'Did I get him?' asked Limpus, tearing at his blindfold.

'No!' screeched his lordship. *'I'm still standing!'*

'Not for long!' screeched Limpet, taking an axe and hurtling it through the air. 'Er Majesty says yer 'ead must come off, and off it will come . . .'

Dungbeetle ducked. Limpus screamed. The axe swooshed over his antennae, catching a drone bee, whizzing through the air, in full haste.

'Pardon?' repeated Limpus, oafishly.

'A Royal Pardon,' murmured the drone bee, feebly.

‘Well, I’m all cut up about this,’ mumbled Limpet, shrugging, watching his lordship, shuffle the long, winding corridor, bemoaning his revenge.

‘You are? What about me?’ murmured the drone, sadly. ‘Will I ever fly again?’

Limpet sighed, remorsefully, ‘Somehow, I donna fink you’ll make der fir’d story.’

Just as Evm Lizard-Wizard had predicted, Queen Bee needed his lordship . . . It seems that, someone, unbeknown to Her Majesty, was pilfering her Royal pots of honey, mysteriously, right under Her Right Royal Nose! Of course, Lord Ruthless Dungbeetle, (apart from organising it himself) knew just the culprit . . . Captain William Kidd Bobbitt. And, as he assured Her Majesty, an utmost cunning plan, to catch this vicious marauder, along with all the crew of the Black Duck, was already formulating.

Captain Bobbitt, woke from his sleep, suddenly. One of his seven senses tingled ominously; why was the *Black Duck* suddenly lame? Worriedly he charged the gangway leading to the poopdeck.

‘Nice day, Cap’n,’ murmured the bosun, a caterpillar named Sammy.

‘Methinks not, Mister Sammy,’ replied Bobbitt, sternly, nose twitching. ‘Wind’s arisin’, southerly.’

‘Gale?’ contradicted the bosun. ‘Yer kiddin’?’ wetting the end of one of his tiny mitts, catching the sickly, warm air.

Bosun Sammy had good reason to doubt; the sea lay calm before a copper-coloured sky; to his untrained eye, that meant fair weather, for the ocean was as clear as crystal.

Bobbitt, for his part put the telescope to his eye and quietly surveyed the dark mass of land that loomed eerily, like a shark’s dorsal fin, before the ship’s bow.

‘Trouble is with you, Mr Sammy, is that you’re still a little green . . .’

‘I am green,’ declared Sammy, ‘I’m a caterpillar. Anyway, what lays yonder island?’ while all hands were busy making fast and dropping the sail.

‘Our destiny,’ declared Bobbitt reluctantly, clutching the locket about his neck, ‘The Crystal Eye.’

'The Crystal Eye,' muttered the crew, becoming motionless statues; stares hung like wraith-like spectres of death, 'Tis cursed, Cap'n.' But before Bobbitt could speak, or even explain, a tremendous squall, sheering, with vicious ferocity, lashed across the midships.

'All 'ands on deck!' barked Bobbitt.

'Make fast all lifelines!' ordered bosun Sammy.

Thunder rocked crag and crevice, the wind whipped and shrilled in ghastly delight as rain pelted and stung Bobbitt's sea-hardened face.

'Keep even keel, Mr Helmsflea,' bawled Bobbitt, trying to rise his voice above the howling, angry wind and the monstrous, battering waves.

'We're losing it,' Cap'n,' bellowed Sammy. 'We're taking water!'

'Not on my watch, Mister,' returned a determined Bobbitt. 'All 'ands bail! *Now!'*

Suddenly, lightning cut the mainmast followed by an ear-piercing shriek. Bobbitt looked round frantically, and saw him, a fellow fleamariner, trapped, lashed against the capstan with the ropes cutting him asunder.

Cutlass, welding the air like a mad dog, he rushed upon him. The fleamariner's eyes nearly popped! 'He's gonna kill me!' he cried.

With one mighty swift blow, the rope split, and the mariner was saved, as for Bobbitt, violently, he was sent skudding across the deck; with a mighty crack of his back and streaming blood from his right eye, groggily he arose, only to hear the bosun's distraught cry, 'Flea overboard!'

With no thought to his own safety, Bobbitt leaped flea metres high and dived out of the sky, straight into pike-infested waters. Home of the notorious pike bandits . . .

As quickly as Sammy gave the order, the lifeboat crashed the sea, somewhere out there, as Bobbitt's blood trickled the storming waters, a few centimetres below, excitement was about to vibrate and ripple the undersea world of Cylous Caesar-pikefish, leader of the pack.

'We 'ave im, Caesar,' reported a gruff and rough, excited Maximus Goblefish-pike. 'Just as you predicted, Sire.'

'Excellent,' Cylous kept saying, gliding round and round, his fearsome fangs, glistening, huge round grey-to-black eyes, glinting menacingly. 'You know the order of battle?' aerial-like eyebrows, knitting, quizzically.

'Sire,' snorted Gobblefish. 'Attack! Sink the *Black Duck!* Gobble up the stragglers!'

'Except Bobbitt!' came a mean and nasty retort. 'He's mine . . . all mine . . .' returning to his clam-cold-stone-throne.

'But that's what I came to report, Sire!' Gobblefish gloated, excitedly. 'Bobbitt, is in the water . . . drowning!'

'What?' bounced the tyrant leader. *'At last!'* Gobblefish-pike beamed, enthusiastically. '*Fetch me my battle dress . . .*'

'Would that be the green-black striped one, Sire?'

Cylous could not believe his luck! He circled round, giggling, thinking of the prize . . . The Golden Locket . . . He was a secret-kinda-fish, on a secret mission . . .

Like a menacing torpedo, he gathered momentum, opening the mouth to let the water in, tingling his gills, then, tilting his head, the vicious-fish, *snapped!*

Bobbitt hastily dragged the fleamariner onto the boat, when a sharp tug nearly sent them sprawling back into the sea. It was as if the ocean itself had suddenly come alive and developed its very own teeth.

Only when he looked at his fellow fleamariner did he realise the truth. 'My goodness,' he gasped, dazed and breathless, 'He's, ate his . . .'

'Leg!' spat Cylous, as the rest of the pike bandits returned from an unsuccessful attack upon the *Black Duck.* All were spitting teeth. All except for Maximus Gobblefish-pike, who'd suddenly realised that something smelt rather 'dungy', about their new leader.

Maximus, suspiciously glided the ocean currents, turning, sharp-fishly. 'You Sire,' he spat, 'are not the fish we think you are, are you?' Cylous, clammed, but on suddenly gulping, an air bubble popped, as did the two of his antennae!

'I thought so,' snarled Maximus. 'Call yerself an emperorfish! Be prepared to be gobbled-in-a-gulp! Maximus, swishing his tail, flew at Cylous, full pelt . . . his mouth opened, his fangs flashed instant death . . .

'*Evm get me outta 'ere!*'

In a flash of onion spry, flip-flopping Dungbeetle was back in his castle, the Forbidden Midden, but before he could lift a mitt to hit the Lizard-Wizard, he squirted onion juice in his eyes.

Dungbeetle, (now back a beetle) blubbered uncontrollably.

'I'm sorry,' he squeaked, wiping his eyes. 'I only wanted the Golden Locket.'

'Sire,' hissed Evm. 'All is not lost, yet, look,' he 'hispered, 'onionating' a vision of Captain Bobbitt. 'See, he comes ashore, upon the Island of Gloom . . . He seeks the Crystal Eye! Alone!' shrieking hysterical laughter. Dungbeetle's eyes, smarted, intensely.

'Oh goody,' sniffled his lordship . . .

The captain, cut off from his ship the *Black Duck,* had never felt so cold, and afraid, warily, with all seven senses tingling alertfulness, wet and weary, he staggered inland, heading to a place he thought he'd find help. A lonely church, where pealed a lonely bell.

Bobbitt, walked the cracked and croaked path, turning his collar, feeling that the bare stubs of burnt-out trees, were watching every move he made; his tiny body shook and shuddered. A grey mist circled the ground, creeping, spiralling, up and up.

He heaved at the solid oak doors. They creaked open. Upon the altar was the prize itself; the woe-bedazzling, Crystal Eye.

Eagerly, Bobbitt surged to take it when, a bloodcurdling eek, resounded the hall. Before him, out of the darkness, stooped a very mysterious, hooded figure.

'What bewitchery is this?' exclaimed Bobbitt, his hand grasping his sword.

'A simple monk,' he slurped, 'a floating whisper, awaiting food.'

Bobbitt relaxed his stance.

'Food? I have none,' confessed he. 'Let me destroy the cursed Crystal Eye, and my crew will bring you some, gladly . . .'

The monk, chortled, 'My food is not your food, captain . . . but my food . . . *is you!'*

The creature, swiftly, caught the captain off guard, and yanked him up in a single claw, that was as sharp as a razor's.

The locked around Bobbitt's neck glowed, intensely.

The creature, threw back its hood, hideously, revealing itself; its eyes as big as saucers, glowered, wickedly, his huge triangular head in wonderment, swayed from side to side, gloatingly.

'Dungbeetle's prize?' Neatly, he snipped the locket's chain. 'And now, your death . . . Bobbitt!'

'What are you?' he gasped, struggling, vainly. The creature roared, ferociously:

‘The Bug’nator!’ mouth opening, fine needle-like teeth, already bloodied.

Bobbitt’s sword, clattered the ground, and then, with an ear-piercing shriek . . . it was over.

‘What now?’ gloated Dungbeetle, happily.

‘The end,’ Evm laughed.

Frinklepops' Family Adventures

(Going to the Fair)

Jackie Davies

The Frinklepops live in a very large chestnut tree on the village green. They are very small people with big brown eyes, long eyelashes, and very thick bushy hair, they have round hands with five fingers and a thumb on each. The extra finger helps them to grip hold of the branches as they climb up and down to their homes.

Frinklemom loves her family very much but sometimes has trouble controlling them when spring arrives and the sap starts rising in the tree. Frinklepop drinks far too much sap which makes him tiddly and he sometimes falls out of the tree, the Frinklepop children laugh so much that they fall out too. Frinklemom gets very cross because she has to keep climbing up and down the tree to get them all and that can be very hard work. She wishes that Frinklepop would set a better example to his children but he never does, he likes the sap too much.

Today they are all going to the country fair, Frinklemom gets the children ready first. There is Frinklepopoose, he is the baby, and Frinklepopple and Frinklepoppy who are twins, they are all very excited about their day out. She dresses Frinklepoppy first as she always stays the cleanest, then Frinklepopoose as he can't walk yet so she can leave him in his cradle, and then Frinklepopple who always get very dirty and is a bit naughty. Frinkepop sits on a branch as usual watching the others and drinking sap. Frinklemom shouts at him to stop

'You won't be able to hold onto the branches to get down if you don't,' she says, but before she has finished saying her words, there is a loud shout, a rustle of leaves and a thud. 'Oh no,' she cries, 'Frinklepop has fallen out of the tree again.'

She decides to leave him on the ground as she gently guides the Frinklepop twins through the branches whilst carrying Frinklepopoose wrapped in a large green leaf and strapped to her back. They all climb down the rope ladder to the ground, where Mom stands and stares at Pop who is lying on his back, arms and legs apart, a big smile on his face and a very large lump on his head. She knows he's not going to the fair now.

'You naughty Frinklepop,' she shouts, 'you've had too much sap again, I told you, and now you have another bump.' *Oh what's the use,* she thinks, 'Come on children, let's go to the fair,' and they all disappear down the track leaving Pop to sleep off the sap.

The fairground is heaving with people and the sound of throbbing music, laughing children and the fair's merry-go-round, everyone is so happy. Because the Frinklepops are so small they must be careful not to get trodden on, especially the twins, so Mom warns them of the danger and tells them to be extra careful, everyone looks like a giant to them, one false move and that could be fatal.

Frinklepopple stares in amazement as a man throws a ball at a coconut, he can't quite believe his eyes. *What a funny thing to do,* he thinks, the coconut topples to the floor, *I wonder if the fairground man will be very cross,* he thinks.

The fairground man just picks up the coconut and hands it to the man who has knocked it on the floor. The man who knocked it onto the floor, then gives it to a smiling little boy and they walk away, hand in hand.

'I wish Frinklepop was here,' says Frinklepopple looking up to Mom. 'Oh dear,' he cries, 'Mom, Mom where are you?' He runs frantically around dodging shoes and heels, 'Mom, where are you?' Suddenly, he feels a great pain rush through his body and is sent hurtling through the air, he'd run in front of someone's boot, they hadn't seen him and had accidentally kicked him, Mom had warned about this happening.

He seemed to fly through the air forever before he fell plonk, straight into a teacup.

This teacup was on a fairground ride and spins him quickly around and around. With being so small there is nothing to hang onto so he gets banged about terribly. Then it all stops and with great difficulty Frinklepopple hauls himself out of the teacup, rolls off the ride and onto the grass. He hurts all over and has an awful headache.

He calls desperately for his mom but she isn't there, he is hurting and is very frightened. He looks all around for somewhere safe to hide, as he doesn't want to be kicked again, and spots a broken flowerpot. Clutching his head and gently sobbing he climbs through the crack, curls up even smaller and falls fast asleep.

Meanwhile Frinklemom, who is so enchanted with a man selling chestnuts, has not yet missed Frinklepopple. *These grow on our tree,* she thinks, *if he can sell them so could I, but how would I get them to the fairground?* They were quite heavy, she would only manage two or three at a time and she couldn't rely on Frinklepop, he was always drinking sap. Well, she decided she would think about this and maybe next year she would have worked out how to do it. The Frinklepops used chestnuts for furniture, they come in all different shapes and sizes and made wonderful tables and chairs.

Frinklepopoose begins to cry, he is ready for a feed so Frinklemom looks for somewhere quiet to feed him. Frinklepoppy is in awe of it all and quietly follows Mom who sits down on a pebble and begins to feed Popoose with the tiniest bottle you have ever seen. Poppy sits on the nearest thing to her, which just happens to be an upturned flowerpot. Suddenly, she hears a tapping noise, she can't see anything, but there it is again. She leans over and raises her dress just enough to gaze inside the flowerpot and there, to her surprise is Frinklepopple, rubbing the sleep from his eyes and knocking the flowerpot sides as he is doing so.

'Good gracious me,' says Frinklepoppy, 'what are you doing in there Popple?'

'I think I got kicked and then bumped my head. I couldn't find you, and then I must have fallen asleep.'

'Well, you're alright now,' said Poppy, 'so don't cry anymore.'

Mom finishes feeding baby, puts him on her back again and takes all three children for tea in the large marquee. It is enormous and the smell of cakes is wonderful.

'You two take these dock leaves and go under the table and get some cake crumbs for our tea,' she says, 'cake crumbs are like fairy cakes to Frinklepops.'

The children obey although Popple is very sore and they duly return with leaves full.

'Now,' says Frinklemom, 'look for as many straws as you can under the small tables the drops of juice left in them will quench your thirsts.'

Again the twins disappear under the tables. Popoose lies asleep while the twins stuff themselves on cake and juice, Mom smiles as she lovingly watches over her children, taking a small crumb and a sip of juice every now and then. *What a lovely day,* she thinks and is happy that her children seem to be enjoying it too.

Glancing down at her tiny watch, she thinks they should perhaps go home now, *Frinklepop will have woken by now and will probably have a sore head.* She knows he deserves it but she loves him very much and is concerned that he is alright. The twins rise to their feet and obediently follow Mom who is once again carrying Popoose on her back. They walk along the track, Popple is tired and a little the worse for wear bruises are beginning to appear on his legs and his bottom hurts too. He is not quite sure what has happened to him so decides not to say anything about it yet, in case Frinkelmom is cross.

Mom notices he is a little quiet and asks, 'Are you alright Popple?'

'Yes I'm fine Mom,' he replies trying not to cry again.

Their tree house is magnificent, especially in summer when it has all of its beautiful green leaves. Mom smiles at its beauty as she approaches and then gently climbs the tiny rope ladder. The twins follow wearily behind and on reaching home, run for their beds and fall fast asleep. Mom puts Popoose in his cradle which is actually an abandoned birds' nest. The birds make these nests each year to have their children in and when their own babies have flown, they kindly let Frinklemom use them for her babies. The nests are extremely cosy and warm for babies and children and she is very grateful to the birds. In return for this favour, she always makes sure that they have enough caterpillars and grubs to eat throughout the winter months when snow is on the ground and food is scarce.

She then went to look for Frinkelpop, he had managed somehow to climb back up the tree to their house and was now snoring his head off once more. *Very full of sap no doubt,* she thinks but is pleased that he is alright and sleeping it off even if he does make her cross sometimes. She gently covers him with a small branch then with a giggle, gives him a kiss on the bump on his head and creeps quietly back to her room.

She collects some rain from a small shell that she keeps on a branch by the kitchen door and makes herself some tea in her favourite thimble. She then settles down on her acorn chair for a well-earned rest, and as darkness falls and tiny stars begin to appear in the night sky she gently drifts off to sleep, knowing that all is well once more with the Frinklepops.

A Country Star

Martin Lee Jackson

Life at Park Avenue Hall is to become sparkled by some live music by the modern legend of country music. At the moment, the name is to be kept secret until the plans are made by the Park Avenue Hall live entertainment manager, Mr Simmons.

Mr Simmons is in his mid 50s, clean-shaven and has straight black short hair. His eyelashes match his hair colour. He is a lively person who socialises a lot with Park Avenue hall, spending the majority of his time in his office, on the telephone, making contracts with famous singers, local theatre companies and local talent show hosts. He is also the bingo caller and poem reciter on the Poet Nights, that are only organised once every month, usually at the beginning of the month (the first Monday night at 8pm).

Katherine Tomkinson, who has beige long streaked hair and pale vixen-look face, is a long-standing and enthusiastic country music fan. She is 18 years old and has just become an assistant to Mr Simmons. She thought about asking him if he would organise a country music night this year.

'Sounds exciting!' Katherine also said, 'there are a lot of young country music fans who come to the line dancing nights you organised every second Friday night here at 8.30pm, whom I host as the Line Dancing Co-ordinator.'

'Yes! You are right! We should do something. I have an idea. Reel me some country music singers, please!' Mr Simmons asked.

Katherine paused to think the request over. In about five minutes, she came up with someone.

'Oh! Sounds good! I will book her in,' John Simmons decided. He immediately went in the office after talking on the hall stage. he grabbed his telephone, dialled a number and got through straight away.

'Would you come next Saturday night at Park Avenue City Hall, in New York at 6.30pm to do a country music live show?'

The singer replied, 'I will just consult my diary.'

Mr Simmons fumbled with his pencil whilst waiting.

The singer said, 'Consider it booked. How long do you want it to be? I do 30 minute slot, one hour slot, two hour slot or four hour slot, at the most.'

John made his mind up and told her to book it for two hours. She wrote the details down and replied with the invoice cost.

'At $100 an hour, plus travel costs at $1 a mile, you will have to pay $297 for the night.'

'Sounds reasonable to me. I will take it.'

The singer gave him instructions to consult her website to make the order and credit card payment. He went on the website and made the payment pronto. Katherine was waiting in the corridor, when he came out and said, 'She's coming!'

Katherine was so please because she was a fan of the singer.

'So what will you charge for ticket cost?' she asked.

John Simmons looked at her and then came up with an answer, 'I reckon $20 per adult, $10 for children and concessions. I will need to make an order with the city council for a live entertainment licence on that night. I will need to contact the local rag to make posters, adverts and also contact New York City radio to advertise the event.'

'Oh!' Katherine was getting even more excited. 'I will contact a shop to get some novelty items to display in the hall,' Katherine suggested.

'Like what?' Mr Simmons had a puzzled expression on his face.

'A saddle, some tankards, some real horseshoes, some large theatre sized American flags to drape either side of the stage, some small American flags to sell on the night. Not forgetting, some Stetson hats!' She went on and on.

'Great! That should spark the right atmosphere with the customers and the singer. She will love that,' he agreed with her proposal.

'Please use the hall budget card for purchasing the items.' She nodded her head and took the card he handed to her, after fetching it from the office safe.

The country music singer event was called 'A Country Star!' It was Saturday, and John expected a large takings for tickets and soft drinks. The hall does not have a bar or have a license to sell alcohol. Still, he was hopeful, considering who the singer was. The posters had a large picture of the singer with the details printed below in red and blue.

At last, Saturday has come, and it is 6pm. The singer has already arrived and set up her equipment on the stage. She has gone back stage to get dressed and apply make-up.

The hall has seats all around but a space in the centre for line dancers. Each seat has a Park Avenue City Hall event calendar. The singer has a table prepared at the back, ready to display her merchandise for selling. She expects some takings from that.

I guess you all readers are still wondering who the singer is? Well, in a story like this, one idea is to keep readers guessing for a bit longer. The climax will be worth the wait, I assure you.

The customers started coming in at 6.30pm. They were flocking in, paying at the door for the ticket and showing their tickets that they paid for in advance. They grabbed a seat, and waited. Drinks were not planned to be served until half time. There was a large selection of drinks, such as orange juice, lemonade, Coca-Cola, coffee, tea, biscuits, crisps and cakes.

As the doors closed at 6.45pm, John Simmons appeared on the stage after walking through the crowd.

'Hello and welcome to the first live country music event in The Park Avenue City Hall calendar called 'A Country Star' and what a star we have tonight. She is well known in the modern country scene, and a legend on internet radio station, www.bluegrasscountry.org! She has sold more than a million copies of her CDs, and the popular one will be sold here, after the show, on the merchandise table when the singer will personally collect your money for the CD and sign the CD if requested.'

Some children were sitting on the floor, playing clapping games with each other. The adults were on the edge of their seats, getting impatient for the show with bulging blue eyes.

John continued, 'Let me not prolong the suspense any longer, and let me take this huge pleasure and ask you to clap your hands to welcome Sheryl Crow to the stage!'

As John jumped off the stage, Sheryl walked fast onto the performing spot on the stage from back stage, with her Stetson hat in her left hand, and a microphone in her right hand. She began her first number with a popular track from 'The Very Best of Sheryl Crow' CD, called 'My Favourite Mistake'. The audience stopped clapping and started listening while Sheryl sat on her chair at the front of the stage, when she place her Stetson hat back on her head and grabbed her black microphone with both hands. She sang the song all the way through, with no interruption from anxious kids who cannot sit still.

As she finished her first song, the audience began to applaud and clap, with a few screams thrown in. The atmosphere was electric.

Sheryl Crow stood up and stepped off the stage. She walked close to the kids who were running around the dance floor. She stopped a child and shook hands.

'Do you know who I am?' she asked,

The kid shook her head from side to side, and then nodded her head. 'You are Dolly Parton!' the kid shouted.

'No! I am Sheryl Crow. I have come here from Las Vegas to sing for you tonight. I would welcome you to come on stage and sing with me. Will you do that?'

The kid was shy, and tucked her head in.

'Yep!'

'Great! What is your name, kid?' Sheryl asked.

'Rachael! Rachael Thorn!'

'Well, Rachael Thorn, I have a song sheet with the lyrics to my next song from the same album. It is called 'Leaving Las Vegas', which I did to come here. I welcome any of you to line dance to this music. Just copy me and my assistant, Rachael Thorn!' She paused to give Rachael the song sheet.

Sheryl sat on the edge of the stage, with Rachael beside her.

'Before we begin, let me welcome you all personally to my live concert, thank you for coming. Drinks and food will be served at half time. I will be selling my merchandise on the table near the exit doors, and if you wish, I will sign your CD or tape. Let me tell you a short story about this next song.' Sheryl sat comfortably with her microphone in her left hand. 'When I was five, my parents took me to Las Vegas to live, and I enjoyed the years we stayed at the city apartment block, near the casinos and night clubs. When I was 18, I did my first gig, at a night club called 'ClubFM', which has an internet radio station, now by the same name. The audience took a shine to me and asked for more, when I finished singing 'All I Wanna Do'. Then, when I was 21, my folks left Las Vegas to live in Los Angeles. I went with them, for a while. I missed Las Vegas night lights and live dance music, but I began a career singing country music at a bar in Las Vegas. The doors were saloon type, and the barman traditionally slid glasses along the bar, like in the country and western films. He remembered when I was 18 at the nightclub because he was there. He asked me, 'Why did you leave Las

Vegas?' I said to stay close to my parents. Then, it inspired me to write a song about leaving Las Vegas hence the title of my next song. Please feel free to sing along and line dance.'

Sheryl started to step to the left, step to the right, skip two steps forward and slid diagonally towards the back and to the right. Rachael copied Sheryl, and then some of the audience stood up, and followed the steps. Sheryl repeated the steps again whilst singing.

Sheryl knelt down so she was at Rachael's height, when she moved the microphone close to Rachael's mouth when they both sang, 'Leaving Las Vegas'! She did this with every chorus.

Each verse had a different line dance routine which made this song difficult to learn to dance to. However, they tried their best after bumping into each other and knocking some of the audience off balance.

'Sorry, Sir! Sorry, Madam,' were the polite comments that were said all through this dance.

Sheryl clapped her hands when she hopped backwards two paces, slid left, slid right and quick jumped forward for the third verse. She repeated this routine all through the verse and then went back to the original routine for the fourth and last verse.

When she finished singing with Rachael, she shook Rachael's hands and said, 'Thank you, Rachael for singing and dancing with me. I hope you will dance on the dance floor for some of my other songs throughout the night.'

Rachael nodded her head and said, 'Yes!'

Sheryl sat back on her chair and sang a tribute for Tammy Wynette called 'Stand by Your Man'.

Sheryl had already told the audience to dance if they want to but Sheryl sat on her chair until the last verse, when she stood up, placed the microphone on the stand, when she twirled and did a few high claps during the twirls. The audience followed suit.

It seemed that everybody was enjoying themselves. The children danced, some couples danced, and some pensioners danced too, wearing beige Stetson hats that they bought in advance of the show.

Sheryl's voice was magic with her next hit, 'Soak up the Sun' that she sung whilst standing behind the microphone stand that supported the microphone. She propped her hands on her hips. Her characteristic country voice was the key that sold more than expected tickets. Mr

Simmons was so pleased that he booked Sheryl Crow, and was so sure that he would book her again in the near future.

'Every Day is a Winding Road' got the audience roaring out the lyrics when Sheryl danced amongst the audience, shaking hands with them as they passed.

The intermission break was planned now, when Sheryl said, 'Please get your drinks and food in this break and I will see you in 20 minutes with my next song, 'The First Cut is the Deepest'.'

Everyone swarmed near the drinks table and food tables. All the drinks and food were free, as paid by the ticket cost. Rachael grabbed a Coca Cola and packet of plain crisps whilst others went for coffee, tea and jammy cakes.

20 minutes went fast when the audience had taken their hot drink cartons back to the tables and sat back for Sheryl's next song that she just told them before the break. Sheryl sat in her chair with the Stetson on the floor, beside her. Instead of the Stetson, she had a small American flag draped from her right fist whilst the microphone was firmly held by her left hand. She sang, 'I have given all of my heart . . . ' She sang and sang this song, and she came to the chorus. 'The first cut is the deepest. The first cut is the deepest. And when it comes to being lucky, he's first. And when it comes to loving me, he's worse.'

Instrumental music followed by some more verses and repeated chorus. She played this track with her guitar.

The other line dance opportunity with 'A Change Would Do You Good' when Sheryl stood on the stage with her wooden guitar, in front of her supported microphone.

The next song was a country hit that she got permission to sing from Dolly Parton when she sang 'Islands In The Stream'. The audience sat still for this song.

'Run, Baby, Run' was the next song that she announced a line dance routine for. She danced on the stage, with her guitar, in front of her microphone. There was a few screams when Sheryl sang the chorus. The audience were throwing their Stetson hats high up in the air, and catching them, raving their high spirits with joy, happiness and 'good time' moods. Some were waving their USA flags above them.

Sheryl put her guitar down on the stage floor and jumped down onto the dance floor when the audience flocked to their seats, when they noticed that the music stopped. Sheryl began talking, 'Now! As I do with all my concerts, I have a little song quiz with just one question. If you have any of my CD albums or tapes, heard my songs on the radio, or been to any of my other concerts, you will have a fighting chance to answer my question. I have a prize! The first hand that goes up and that person who answers my question correctly will receive a free signed copy of 'The Very Best of Sheryl Crow' CD, a signed small USA flag, and a signed poster.'

There was a pause when Sheryl consulted her piece of paper that she just got from her jeans pocket.

Just before Sheryl poses the question, I will take time out and just describe what Sheryl Crow is wearing tonight. She has her dark blue denim jeans, her cream knitted jumper, her navy slacks and she has pink lipstick, and light pink eye shadow.

Right, now to the question. 'Hello fans out there, and here too. To receive the signed goodies, please tell me the song title that this following lyric line comes from . . . 'I like to watch the sun come up!'

There was silence at first, and the hands shot up. Sheryl had sharp eyes and spotted the first hand.

A blonde woman in her fifties was the first.

'Please stand up!' Sheryl asked.

The woman stood up.

'What's your name?'

The woman spoke her name. 'Megan Roberts.'

Sheryl said, 'What is the answer to my question?'

Megan spoke, 'Home!'

Sheryl looked at Megan with haunting eyes and then said, 'Please come here to the front, Megan!'

Megan obeyed. When Megan reached the front, Sheryl grabbed Megan's left hand and lifted it in the air.

'You are correct! Well Done! You receive my signed goodies. Please just wait there while I get them.'

Sheryl fetched the stuff and gave them to Megan. Megan sat down, and Sheryl got back on the stage, picked her guitar and spoke 'For my last number, I will sing 'Strong Enough'. Please feel free to sing along.' Sheryl plucked her guitar with a spectrum for this song.

Everybody clapped whilst she sang. Some of them sang along. Just as Sheryl placed her guitar down, a man from the audience screamed, 'More! More! More! More!'

Sheryl asked, 'You want more?'

They shouted, 'Yeah! We want more! Encore! Please, Sheryl Crow! More! More!'

Sheryl consulted her watch and said, 'To the hell with it! Any requests?'

There were many hands went up. Sheryl spotted a hand from the back of the hall. Sheryl said, 'What song do you want me to sing for the very last song?'

The child shouted, 'Leaving Las Vegas!'

Sheryl Crow nodded her head in hearing the request. 'Right! The public has spoken! 'Leaving Las Vegas' it is. Feel free to sing and line dance, as before. Before I begin, I would like to thank everyone and each of you for coming tonight and I hope you have seriously enjoyed yourselves! I hope you can buy my merchandise and I hope you can join me with any of my future tours. For my next concert, I am going to New Jersey. I hope you can join me. If not, I hope you can still enjoy my music with the CD, tape or radio stations. Safe ride home and good night!'

Sheryl sat on her chair with the microphone in her right hand and her Stetson in her left hand when she burst into song. Later, she grabbed her guitar and did an instrumental version of the song, followed by a line dance twirl and 'Leaving Las Vegas' chorus line dance traditional routine that all the audience copied, with a reasonable degree of error.

When the music ended, and just before Sheryl walked off the stage she bowed and shouted, 'Good night!'

Mr Simmons walked to the front and asked for the audience's attention. 'Please have a safe ride home, and take the calendar for future live events here in the near future. I hope you get some merchandise of Sheryl Crow. She is selling CDs, tapes, posters, etc. It leaves me to say goodnight and God bless!'

Mr Simmons went back to the doors and opened them, while Sheryl brought her boxes with help by Katherine. She set the merchandise on the table. She spent about 40 minutes selling her stuff, signing the majority of them. Everybody left by 10.15pm.

INFORMATION

We hope you have enjoyed reading this book - and that you will continue to enjoy it in the coming years.

If you are interested in becoming a New Fiction author then drop us a line, or give us a call, and we'll send you a free information pack.

Alternatively if you would like to order further copies of this book or any of our other titles, then please give us a call or log onto our website at www.forwardpress.co.uk

New Fiction Information
Remus House
Coltsfoot Drive
Peterborough
PE2 9JX
(01733) 898101